DREAMS OF
THE HUNT

Michael James Kaufman

D1214966

ISBN: 9798643296539

Independently Published
Cover design: Photo by Eberhard Grossgasteiger.
www.pexels.com/@eberhardgross
Printed in the United States of America

T he afternoon was cold and gloomy. The grays of the clouds faded into the mountains. The sun had been hidden most of the day and the temperature had dropped ten degrees since the morning. This was a typical day for northwestern Montana in the late fall. It was no surprise to Ray Harris either. Ray was an older man. His dirty blonde hair had turned mostly gray and was messy, although he wore a hat most of the time. He had a stocky build like his grandfather, who was a logging man. His face was wrinkled some and showed his age, and the shiny blue in his eyes had changed with time and was much duller now. His beard was full and hung well below his chin. His hands were rough and scarred. One hand was on the steering wheel, and the other held a cigarette. He had quit smoking long ago but wanted one for the trip, so he had bought a pack.

He was going to hunt near Dove Lake and drove by himself in his old Chevy pickup. He was almost to the town of Timber Falls now. He had the window cracked, and the smoke from the cigarette steadily escaped the cab. He had two rifles and a muzzleloader, each in their own cases on the floor behind him. He kept his pistol holstered in the center console. The bench back seat was full of hunting gear. The tarped bed was full of food and supplies, enough for the four days he would be in the mountains. He owned a cabin near Dove Lake with Jim Klevenger. Jim was an old friend he had met in the Navy who had passed away in the summer, and this would be Ray's first time going to the cabin to hunt alone. For the last twenty years, they had gone hunting at least once a year and if not at the cabin, then somewhere else. They sometimes fished, also. That depended too on the season and the weather. The past five years they had gone elk hunting and been wanting to hunt bear. So, Ray was after a bear. He usually hunted bear in the spring, but they had planned the hunt for fall so he was going to stick to that. There was a rush he got when bear hunting. He had not gone in so long, he missed it. He wished he could hunt a grizzly, but they could no longer be hunted in Montana. So, a black bear would have to do. He was not going to do a full bear

mount when he killed one. He planned on field dressing the bear and then bringing the rest back. Almost a third of the weight would be left behind with the guts of the bear. His four-wheeler could be of help if he needed it. He may not be able to get to where the bear was but any bit closer would help.

He loved to hunt and had gone his whole life. It had been his favorite hobby for as long as he could remember, and it gave him a feeling that nothing else did. He

enjoyed the change it brought and the fact that one hunt was never the same as the last. Even when he did not kill anything. Just being in the outdoors and the wild. He thought that maybe it was a primal thing, but he did not care what it was. It was good, and it always helped him clear his mind too, which was the main reason he was going now. He needed the change in pace and new scenery.

"Good old Timber Falls," Ray said.

The town sat quiet, a half-mile ahead as he rounded a corner on the two-lane highway. Pine trees bordered both sides of the road. The town was built on a hill that ran down to the Clark Fork River. To the left, a stretch of tree-covered mountains towered over the hill and town. To the right were the river and more mountains in the distance. The road lead straight on to the main street and along some railroad tracks. The rail was still used but not nearly as much as it once was. Parallel with the tracks was the town's businesses. He had gone through Timber Falls every time he went to the cabin and whenever he was in the area. The old town was familiar to him. He also had some family that lived around the town. When it snowed a good amount in the winter, he and his uncle used to go snowmobiling in the mountains above the town. His grandfather had lived east of the town, so he spent much of his childhood there and that is where he found his passion for hunting and the outdoors. It was a peaceful town and he liked it. He pulled up to the bar and parked his pickup.

The weather isn't bad yet, he thought. It's never good to underestimate the weather, though. Especially in the mountains. I'll stay for a couple like we've always done.

He was thirsty and he had stopped at the bar every time he went through. It was still daylight and he had around two hours of driving left before he made it to the cabin. The bar was as quiet as the town. Two men played a game of pool and another sat alone at the bar. Ray walked in and sat down on a stool. He loved the way it felt to sit at a bar. It brought his spirit up, and even when it was quiet, the atmosphere was still comforting. He could sit there for hours. If it were not for hunting, then drinking at a bar would be his favorite hobby. It was a close second anyways. He did not know if the Navy had started him on that or if he was bound for it no matter what. He thought that it was better than drinking alone. But he did enjoy driving up a mountain road and drinking too. They had called it booze cruising when he was younger. He had also been arrested for it once near Timber Falls. That was in my late twenties, he thought. That was a long time ago.

"Ray! It's good to see you!" the bartender said.

"Hey there. You too."

She was a younger woman, and he could never remember her name. She stepped around the bar and gave him a hug.

"I was sorry to hear about Jim. I'm gonna miss him."

"Yeah, thanks. It's definitely been a quieter trip without him."

"I'm sure it has. Once he would get to talking, he could really go with it. So, you're going up to the cabin to hunt by yourself?""Well you don't have to say it like I'm too damned old. I'm only sixty."

"I didn't mean it like that."

"Sure. Sure."

She handed him a beer.

"Thanks."

"Anything for you, dear."

The mug was frosty, and the beer was gold with some head. He grabbed the handle of the mug and took a drink. The beer stuck to his mustache as he set the mug back down.

"That's better than it's ever been."

"You say that every time."

"That's cause it's always better."

"There's never a dull moment with you."

"Nope, I reckon not. I better do a shot of Jameson too."

"I was already getting that around for you."

"You must remember things better than I do."

"I mean, you are getting up there in age.

"I know it."

"I'm only kidding. Are you hunting bear this year

or what?

"That's the plan anyways."

"Remind me again. Female or male?

"Male. They are actually called boars and sows just like pigs."

"Oh, I didn't know that. Interesting."

"The sows are getting close to or already hibernating by now. Most boars should still be roaming around looking for food. Until the weather gets too bad.

"There is some bad weather coming, you know."

"Yeah, I saw that before I left home, and I was listening to the radio on the way. I have plenty of supplies in my pickup and the cabin. I should make it up there before it gets too bad anyhow."

"Had to stop and see me first, huh?"

"You betcha. One of Montana's finest sites."

"You tend to get sweet with beer."

"And age."

Ray drank his shot and two more beers and thought of memories he had in the bar. He looked at the pictures on the wall. He had known some of the people in the pictures. He thought how crazy time was and where it had taken him. That is all anyone has, is time. They have each other as well, but only for as long as time permits.

Or until people permit, he thought. How many times had Kate come and gone in my life?

Kate was a woman he had met a long time before when they were both young. She lived in northern California, and he had not seen her in a few years.

She had become more like a dream, he thought. She would show up for a smile or two and be gone.

He could have stopped it many times before, but he had loved some women and none compared to her. Kate would never marry him, but they had a son together. After all the years though, he would not ask her anymore. He might ask her, but he would not mean it. He loved her, but he was no longer in love with her. He did not like to talk about her much or relationships for that matter. The rule was no talking about religion or politics and he just added the relationship part in there too. He understood government but not politics. He saw the politicians as lying crooks. As for God, he believed in him but did not like people shoving religion in his face or telling him how to believe. He had his own way. One of the many reasons he missed Jim's company. If Jim talked about religion or politics, he was quick to the point and gave an honest opinion. Jim would never talk much about women either. At least not for long. He and Jim got along splendid.

I miss Jim, he thought. I miss a lot of old, dead friends. Nothing I can do but keep on keeping on. Think of something different, he thought. Think of black bears in the mountains.

They looked magnificent as they roamed through the trees. Their backs looked like rolling black hills and nature seemed to stand still for them to pass by. He respected them as much as he respected every animal he hunted. It was a beautiful thing to respect your adversary. He had not hunted one in six years.

The last time he went was with his son. It was spring then, and the snow had melted, and the rivers were full. He could not remember how big the bear was that his son shot, but it was an average size. He was excited for this year because the bears had been on good food supply all year and the last two winters were short and easy on them. He wanted to get one this trip, more than he ever had before.

I'll get one, he thought. I'll get one.

"How's your welding shop?" the bartender asked.

"It's still there."

He had worked as a welder and fabricator in the Navy and as a civilian. The Navy was good to him, but he never liked it enough to re-enlist. He joined to serve his country and he had done so. That was enough for him. He spent four years in the service and then got out and worked as a welder in the Nevada goldmines. He had lived in Nevada most of his life. When most people thought of Nevada, they thought of Las Vegas. He hated when people asked him if that was where he was from like that was the only city or town in the whole state. He was from northern Nevada and he would let anyone know, that asked. After he worked for the mines long enough, he opened his own shop, which he worked until he retired two years before. Well, semi-retired. He still did some work in his shop because he enjoyed welding and working too much to quit completely. Welding had come easy for him and he had developed a skill for it. He loved the feeling he got when he finished a job or a project. Everyone should get a good feeling of satisfaction when working hard and completing something, he thought. It makes for a better world that way. He especially enjoyed to TIG weld. It took more concentration and muscle movement. The way the arc would melt the filler metal into the material was like watching a raindrop fall into a puddle. Then the arc would straighten the puddle into a fine, perfect weld like a stack of dimes. He enjoyed striving for perfection and he could do that with welding. It was a welcomed relief to the imperfections of life. Times had changed, and modern ways irritated him. People and their technology annoyed him. He had reached the age where he had seen plenty of friends and family die, and he coped with it, but that never made it easier to understand. It was good for him to stay busy for that reason.

"Are you still the best welder around?" the bartender asked.

"I never knew that I was."

"Oh, yes you did. You're just being modest."

"Well, I can still do as good as I always have."

"You're probably better and don't even know it."

"I have gotten better at some things in my old age."

"Oh, have you now? You've probably got the old man wisdom too."

"All that is, is learning from all the mistakes you make over the years. Someone just decided to call living through failures, wisdom."

"I'd say that's still something special to have."

"Yeah, I suppose it is."

Then the rain came. Drops fell onto the window of the bar and slipped their way down in streaks. It was not long before the rain turned to sleet and then to snow. The temperature had dropped into the low twenties. He tipped his mug up and swallowed the last of his beer.

"You best be going if you're going," the bartender said.

"I better."

"You sure you should even go now? It looks worse out there than they said it would be and you won't have much phone service east of here."

"I'll be fine. I don't get any service at the cabin either and it's kind of nice that way. I just like my phone for music."

"I don't think I would like not having service for that long. You could stay here and keep me company."

"I'll be fine, and I'll be seeing you. Hopefully, I'll get a bear so I can show it to you when I come back through."

"I'll have a beer waiting for you. Be safe."

He walked out into the evening. The pure white snow fell into his beard. The cloudy sky held onto the last of what the sun had to give. The air had gotten cold, and the wind blew some. He started his pickup and turned on the radio. He could not find anything but talk shows on, so he played some music on his phone. He waved to the bartender as she looked out the window of the bar. In my younger years, I would have stayed with her, he thought. The streetlights showed how quickly the snow fell and laid the path out of town. A few houses up the hill had Christmas lights, and some did not. The moon had peeked through the packed clouds and shimmered off the flowing river. Out of town, the road started to ice from the earlier rain. The snow began to cover the landscape, and the road wound its way through the mountainous terrain. The river flowed alongside, surrounded by steep jagged rock formations and in some turns, the road was close enough to the mountains for Ray to reach out of his pickup window and touch them. The pass opened and ran parallel with some train tracks. The tracks crossed over the cold river on a wooden bridge that sat just a mile from an old rail station. Pine and fir trees covered the mountains in spots and in others were scarce. Some spots the trees did not look like they belonged at all. Like a lone sheep among wolves.

Then the road left the river and began to climb again and up into the mountains it went. The cabin was up an old logging road that was only passable by one vehicle at a time. The right shoulder was a towering mountain, and the left shoulder was a steep drop off into the trees and down the mountain. The road became treacherous with snow and ice though Ray carried on. He had driven those roads his whole life. He grew up between Montana and Nevada, so he had learned to drive in the mountains and in the winter. Some of his family had told him he should wait until the weather had cleared or for the spring. Men can be stubborn. Ray had lost a friend. His sixtieth birthday was the same month Jim had died. Now it was five months later, and he was not about to end the tradition.

He listened to old country music and watched the road through the busy windshield wipers. The snowflakes were thin. They came down in a hurry and stuck to the ground below. He could tell that the road was slick, and he slowed down a bit. I've seen it worse than this, he thought. The pickup lights shined through the snow, and it looked like a billion stars. He could see the rocky wall and each sharp edge that stuck out towards the road. He was on the most dangerous part of the road, and he knew that. The guard rail was faulty for a half-mile due to erosion on the edge of the shoulder. He sang along with the music and drove into the snowy night. He rounded a corner, and the pickup tail whipped some, but he corrected it. Then, around the next curve, a herd of mountain goats was standing in the middle of the road. He stepped on the brake pedal and then let off. The pickup went sideways. He tried to correct it, and then he stepped on the brakes again. The goats stood still and stared at the head-lights. He barely missed the goats but neared the edge of the road and turned hard. He closed his eyes.

That was damned close, he thought. Not even bad weather or a wreck could keep me from this hunt.

The road would flatten out ahead, and the shoulder was no longer steep. The forest covered each side of the road and stretched out down into a valley and up into the mountains. The cabin was a dependable cabin tucked away in the forest near the lake. He owned the cabin and five acres around it. There were other houses up and down the road but none nearby. The moon lit up the big sky, and the snow danced down between the trees and onto the roof. A soft breeze carried the fresh mountain air through the cold evening. The darkness had a purple tint to it. Like a dream would have. Ray had never seen it look like that before.

"It sure is beautiful," he said. "Wish you were here Jim."

Wolves howled in the distance. Ray gave out a loud call himself.

Just an old wolf, he thought. A lone wolf for sure. Old for sure.

He carried his gear and supplies into the cabin. He filled the generator with fuel and got it running. The cabin was used by his relatives and friends quite often, so everything was well-kept. He put his muzzleloader on the rack and packed his bag for the next day's hunt. There were pictures in the cabin from different trips elsewhere and to the cabin. From the time they fished in Alaska, hunted whitetail in Iowa, and countless other trips and places. The moose Ray killed ten years before was mounted in the gun room. A bear rug lay in the middle of the living room. It was the bear his son had killed.

He watched the snow out the window and sat down on his chair. He loved being in the mountains. They made him think of younger times and all the memories he had made in them. Since he had retired, he had thought about moving to them for good. If it were not for his shop at home, he would. Next to being out on the open ocean, the mountains were his favorite place to be.

The cabin was cold. He started a fire in the fireplace and got his wood stove burning. That warmed it up quick and made the whole inside smell sweet. The pine wood always smelled sweet to him. It was a messy wood when burned but he did not mind. Nothing about the outdoors or camping bothered him. I love it out here, he thought. He knew some folks that never liked staying up in the mountains, for hunting or for vacation. He never understood that. The winters could be terrible, but if they had enough supplies, then there was no worry. There was plenty of running water all around the cabin from the rivers and streams. If he were to stay forever, he would like to have plumbing, though. For the few days that he stayed to hunt, it never bothered him to use the outdoors as a restroom.

I guess I'm biased, he thought. It's understanding that some people don't want to be a mountain man just like I don't want to live in a city.

He decided to cook some venison. He always had venison with vegetables. He always had beer too. Not with his meal though. It took away the taste of the food and the beer and he did not like that. After supper, he turned on some music and drank beer.

"How about some Lucero," he said. He sat back

down in his chair and put a pinch of tobacco in his mouth.

He sang aloud with the music. The night had settled in and so had Ray. The snow continued to fall as he sang and drank in the cabin. What a night to start this hunt, he thought. He hoped that the snow would slow down and not be too deep in the morning. Maybe I should pray for better weather, he thought.

"Like God cares about my hunting trip," he said. He laughed out loud. Bad weather or not, he thought. I'll find a bear.

The morning came and the sun shed light on the snow that had fallen. The clouds had dissipated, and the sky looked as though it went on forever. He was glad to see that the snow was not terribly deep and could be managed. He had thought about going out to hunt in the early morning, but he drank a little more than he had intended. He would wait till late afternoon. That would be the best time for him to find a bear. He made some coffee and sat around while he drank it.

The cabin roof was covered with snow and the green of the trees was barely visible. The air was crisp and clean and animal tracks were the only marks in the fresh snow. There was a peaceful quiet. He liked that about the mountains. They were usually quiet. The mountains and the oceans. Natural and elegant.

He made himself a breakfast with his coffee. The bacon crackled on the skillet, and that reminded him of welding. He made eggs in the bacon grease like his grandfather had taught him when he was younger. The cabin smelled of firewood and breakfast. One of the best smells around, he thought. He felt better after he ate, but his head still hurt.

Fresh air is always nice for a hangover, he thought. He went outside and looked around. The morning sun hit his face, and the air took his breath for a moment. The cold air blew like smoke from a chimney with each of his breaths. The snow crunched with every step, and he was worried about the noise he would make later when he walked. He did not want to scare any potential game.

I'll have to be quiet, he thought.

He walked around back and opened the door to the utility shed behind the cabin.

"There she is," he said.

He grabbed an axe and swung it up on his shoulder.

There is nothing quite like a man and his axe, he thought. A man and his dog maybe. Or his cat. Cats could be good. He thought of Jameson and Marlboro. They were his two cats back home. They were not as needy as dogs. He liked that about them. A man and his gun, too, he thought. He sometimes talked to his guns when cleaning them or when on the hunt.

The log pile in the run-in shed was big enough, but he wanted to cut wood for fun more than for need. He found some that needed split and set them up. The axe looked like it belonged in his hands, and his hands looked at ease holding the axe. The first whack sent a jolt through the trees and scared a few birds up into flight. He would split a piece of wood and then grab another and put it on the tree stump and then swing again. He chopped the wood for a long while until streams of sweat ran down his face and into his beard. He removed his maroon flannel coat and then wrapped his hands back around the handle of the axe and kept at the work. He found it easier to keep going at his age than he did when he was younger. Maybe it was because he was not in any sort of hurry. There was not as much on his mind, he was content. Or maybe he was just stronger than he used to be. Old man strength, he thought. That is what he called it. His stepfather had it when Ray was young. He had always admired that about him. There's something about a man that works hard and never complains, he thought. That says a lot about a man's character. I don't think you see that as much anymore, he thought.

The pile of split wood mounted up. He laid the axe down and caught his breath before he picked up the split pieces. His forearms were tight and his back hurt some, but he was used to that. He rubbed his back with his calloused hands and cursed the pain under his breath.

The work had made him hot, and the sunshine warmed him up as well. There were no clouds in the sky, and some of the snow on the tops of the trees began to melt. Though in some places, the snow on the ground came up to his shins. The temperature had gotten above freezing and stayed there, and it looked more like spring than late fall.

He went inside and got his lever-action rifle. He had decided that he was going to hunt a rabbit or two for lunch. He had brought meat on ice and put it in the freezer but had not had rabbit in a long time and wanted to try it for old time's sake. The taste was nothing to brag about, but he liked to hunt his food. It would not be difficult at all to find rabbit tracks, but to find the rabbit, he did not know. He never knew with rabbits. Before he left, he fixed up the stove so it would burn for much of the day. He always remembered to do that. It was far better to come back to a warm cabin. Once he was ready to go, he put on his pack and sheathed his knife on to his belt and holstered his pistol. It was a 44. Magnum.

"My sweet Anne," he said. "I hope you're as ready for this trip as I am. I know you are."

Ray was a big fan of many weapons, but the pistol was his favorite firearm. He always carried a knife and pistol as secondary weapons. He always carried his pack too, no matter how long he planned to be out. Anything could happen. There were wolves and big cats and not just black bears but brown bears too.

He stepped back outside, and the sun met him at the door. He squinted at the bright snow between the trees. Should have brought my sunglasses, he thought.

"I'm just glad that it's warming up," he said.

He trudged out through the trees away from the cabin. The sun was almost at its highest point for the day. The wind had stayed calm all morning but picked up a little. An eagle flew between two trees in front of him and watched him as it circled around and up onto a tree.

"I'm not killing anything for you," he said. "Unless you lead me to a black bear in the next couple days. Then I'll even give you some of it. How would that be? Yeah, you'd be as happy as a pet coon, and so would I."

The mountain peaks laid out behind him in the distance as he walked up a hill through the deepest snow he had seen. It came up to his knees, and he hoped that it would only be that way on that hill. It was a tough climb, so he was winded by the time he reached the top, and the depth of the snow lessened. I'm out of breath already, he thought. Moisture had stuck to his facial hair and made the hairs around his mouth look like miniature icicles. He was glad to be in shallow snow as he walked down a slope into a clearing. It was the first time he had gotten a clear look at the sky since he had left the cabin. It's the Big Sky alright, he thought. Then he looked down over the hills, and he could see the lake now. It was bigger than it had ever seemed to him before. It was an odd shape that would be hard to explain without drawing it on a piece of paper. The lake was not frozen but looked like glass, and although he was far up and away from it, he could see the reflection of the mountains. Beneath the mountains, the lake was surrounded by trees as far as he could see.

"Maybe I'll go down to the lake this trip," he said. It gets prettier every time I'm out here, he thought.

He saw all kinds of tracks in the snow. There was hardly an inch of snow anywhere that had not been touched by an animal. He found some rabbit tracks and tried to follow them but could not. He saw some brush and went that way. He hoped that he could step around and scare one or two out. The brush was down the hill in front of him, and the snow crunched at each of his steps. He had caught his breath, and the downhill walk was easy. A rabbit jumped up out of the brush and hopped around a couple of trees to his right. He put his rifle to his shoulder but did not have a clear shot.

"Damnit!" he said. "I'll get him."

He followed along the same path that the rabbit had made. He was not far behind. He saw the rabbit bounce between trees but could not keep his eyes on it.

Where did it go? he wondered.

He stopped and listened. The forest was quiet. He stroked his beard for a moment and looked for the rabbit. Nothing. He continued to walk. The cold air bit at his nose and started to turn it red. He never minded the cold. Jim had hated the cold. He thought of how much his friend had hated the cold and the last time they hunted in the mountains in the early spring.

Ray and Jim had walked all day and took a rest atop a clearing on a rock.

"That damn wind is cold," Jim said.

"Yeah, it is. You need a thicker beard."

"Are you making fun of my beard? It's a good beard."

"Maybe for the summer."

"I don't spend as much time in the Rockies as you. It hasn't had the time to develop."

"That could be it."

"I've got to take a leak," Jim said. "I can't get to anything with these gloves on either. The damn thing is gonna be shriveled up and hard to find."

Then Ray remembered that he talked about how cold his hands were after that. He chuckled at the memory.

He walked on and found a narrow trail where the snow had sunken into. He remembered the area and knew exactly where he was. There were rabbit tracks all over, but he still had not seen the one that came from the brush. He walked along the trail and looked up at the sun. It warmed his chilled face, and there were still no clouds in sight. It was about noon, and he was hungry and thirsty.

I haven't seen a damn thing but that one rabbit, he thought. I've already wandered far enough. A little further, and I'm going back and eating some more deer meat. It's better anyhow.

He headed downhill, and there was no sign of any small game, just their tracks. Plenty of birds flew by and talked to one another but nothing else. He had gone further than he intended. He paid no attention to the tracks as he thought a lot, and it passed the time without him knowing. Hunting was hardly on his mind. He thought of his son and his grandkids. He would have asked his son to come with him, but he had wanted to do this alone. He had talked to Jim before he died, and they had planned the trip for late fall. So, Ray did not want to miss it, and he did not want to replace Jim. Not that it would be replacing him, he thought. And he knew that Jim would not care, but it just felt wrong to him to take someone else. His back hurt, and he had missed a chance at a rabbit.

That's why I continue questioning doing this trip alone, he thought. The weather had gotten bad before, but it was nice now. I have nothing to complain about, he told himself. I'm not dead.

The mountains were as beautiful as he had ever seen, and the sun had been out all day, making the temperature more than bearable. He wiped the moisture from his mustache and rubbed his lower back. To hell with the pain, he thought. That is just part of getting old. He stopped and listened, and then started walking again in the same direction he had been, and then over the crunch of his steps, he heard running water.

"You snuck up on me," he said to the river.

It was a small river with a quick set of rapids. The area where he neared the water was more of a creek. The width was only ten feet. He walked along the bank and could see up ahead where the water widened out, and the rapids started. Trees were scattered around the area and still had some of the night's snow on them. The bank was just above the water but got higher and steeper as it widened. Rocks jutted out and exposed themselves through the layer of snow. He followed the bank along towards the noisy rapids. Three large peaks showed above the trees behind him, and they were covered white and looked as harsh as the coming winter. He stopped not far from the rapids and looked across the river. The opposite bank looked identical to the side he stood on. He set his pack down and stretched his back and moved his legs around. He had walked a considerable distance from the cabin but still knew his way back. I could make it back to the cabin with my eyes closed, he thought. He removed his gloves and got his water from his pack and took a drink. The water was cold, but it felt good on his lips and down his throat. He took another drink, and some water dripped down the corner of his mouth and into his beard. He gazed at the river and the opposite bank downstream.

"What was that?" he asked out loud.

He looked across the river intently.

"That looked like Jim!" he said. "Or it looked like me." We don't even look alike, he thought. Jim is taller and leaner. "Then what or who was it?"

He felt a chill run over his body.

There's no way that was him, he thought. And I'm standing here. What or who could it have been then?

He put his water away and left his pack and walked along as fast as he could through the snow.

His rifle was in his hand at his side, and he watched for anything to move across the river. He knew that Jim was dead, but he saw something.

It was a person, he thought. It looked like Jim, but it couldn't have been him.

The other bank was still. He did not know if he was seeing things or if there was something. His eyes shifted about in a calm frenzy. He never got too excited, so even when he was startled, his demeanor was relaxed. There was no noise except for the rapids and his thoughts. He stopped and tried to listen more. He looked back upstream at the thin part of the river.

I could cross there, he thought. Why would I cross? I'm seeing things. I'm not chasing an imaginary figure across this river.

Just then, his feet slipped beneath him. He had stepped on false ground over the bank and fell through the snow. The fall was not far, but it was not graceful. He fell backward and sharply onto the bank. Then he went head over feet and smashed his head on a rock as he dropped his rifle and rolled into the water. The rifle sank into the water and disappeared. The rock hit just above his right eye, which started to bleed immediately. The water was ice cold and soaked through his winter clothing. It was deep enough and moved enough to slowly carry him out into the current. The collision had nearly knocked him out. He was on his back, and a stream of blood ran down his face and into the river ahead of him.

What the hell happened? he wondered. Was that Jim across the river? How the hell did I get in the water?

The sunshine made him blink. He felt the blood over his eye. He noticed the cold of the river on his bare skin, and it soaked through his clothes and his muscles twitched. The water got rougher. He was getting close to the rapids. He turned over in the water and began to swim to the side. He was not sure how deep the water was, but the current moved him faster and faster and was too strong for him to stop and try to stand. The rapids would beat him up more than his spill into the river had, and they were getting ever closer. He saw a large rock that sat in the river alone and reached out for it. It was enough to grab ahold of. He got his feet below him, but he still could not stand. The water got deep in a hurry, he thought. He laid over the rock and tried to catch his breath. Blood dripped from his head and washed down onto the rock. The cold had reached his entire body, and he shivered.

I've got to get to the river's edge, he thought.

He took a few more deep, shaky breaths and pushed hard off the rock. The current fought him as he struggled to swim through it. He felt the bottom on his feet, so he stood and waded through until he reached the shore and pulled himself up onto the bank. The snow clung to his wet clothes and body. He cursed himself for falling into the river. The water was freezing on his hands, and they were so cold he could barely bend his fingers.

"I dropped Doc," he said. That was the name he had given his lever-action rifle. That was a damned foolish thing to do, he thought. I've got to get up and get moving.

He got to his knees and looked at his blood in the snow. He was shaking and trying to keep his mind positive, and he tried to keep moving. The river kept on as if nothing had happened. He stumbled back up-river and got to his pack. He removed his hat, and his hair stiffened. He cursed himself for not having his gloves on, and his hands had turned red and stung with pain, so he rubbed them together for warmth. He took his clothes off as quickly as he could and slipped his boots back on. The air cut into his wet, naked body. His pistol was still in its holster, and his knife was still on his belt. He was grateful for that. He packed the clothes in his bag and wrapped himself up in his thermal blanket. I knew this blanket would come in handy someday, he thought. Then he threw his belt over one shoulder and the pack over the other. They both did a good job of keeping the blanket on him. The cold was now a part of him, and he could not stop shivering. His feet were like ice blocks in the boots. He took one more look across the river. Then he started to jog back the way he had come, back to the cabin. His legs did not want to move, and he felt like he was moving two of himself.

The snow seemed deeper to him, and the air much colder now. He moved through the timber as quickly as he could. He hoped to see smoke from the cabin but knew that he was still a far cry away. It would cheer him up to see the smoke. He tried his best to follow his path from before but strayed some. It was much easier to walk through the dense woods when he was on the path. His walk was more of a shuffle than a walk. A streak of blood had frozen from his wound down over his eyebrow and cheek. Ice had formed all over his beard and hair.

His head hurt from the cold, and his hands had gone numb. He thought of warmer times. The memories he had of the Pacific. He remembered walking outside in the early morning, and the humidity would meet him like a strong wind. He would be sweating before he had even done anything. He disliked it then but would love it now. The sun would beat down like its only purpose was to burn him and him alone. Even when the sun was hidden, the days were warm and humid. He thought of the hot days he spent welding parts for submarines in the shop on his ship. How hot it was. The sweat. He tried to feel that. He remembered when he and Jim had to do some welding inside the waste tank on a submarine. It was empty, of course. The ship was anchored, and the submarine was on the other side of the pier. They carried their gear down off the ship and across the pier. The walk was hot, and the gear was heavy. The submarine looked like a log floating in the water, and the crew moved around on the deck and below, looking like ants resupplying their hill. The passageways and scuttles through the sub were smaller than movies had made them look, and there was only enough room for one person to walk. They made their way through the mazelike passageways and crawled through pipes and more scuttles and squeezed into the waste tank. Their equipment was a burden and so was the smell. But it was warm. He remembered it like it had just happened. He could still smell the tank and hear the conversation he and Jim had.

"What a shitty deal we've gotten ourselves in," Jim said.

"No doubt."

"I guess it beats listening to Chief talk about things that don't matter and coming up with things to do that don't make sense."

"That's for sure. We're due a good chief."

"I'd say we are."

"At least there are decent leaders here and there."

"Few and far between."

"Another positive note, we could be stuck doing random training or a fire drill."

"Hey, last fire drill, I was securing boundaries and put the fire out with an extinguisher, and it was over quick."

"Those are the best drills, over quick."

Ray remembered the smoke being sucked through the ventilation hose and the smell it caused as he started welding. The welder made the tank even hotter and the smell even worse.

"I miss being out to sea," Jim said.

"Same here. There's nothing else like it."

"Look at us, always wanting to be doing what

we're not doing."

"They say a bitching sailor is a happy sailor."

"I suppose it's not all bad."

"At least we can agree that we'd much rather be down in this shit tank welding than back on the ship doing something else."

"Yes, agreed."

The job took them two workdays to complete, and most of both days were spent in the tank. Their uniforms smelled like the tank, and no amount of washing would fix that. They were sweaty and hot by each day's end, but they enjoyed the job. Ray remembered how at ease he was and how warm it was. The warmth most of all.

The cold air nipped at his body, and he stumbled through some deep snow but caught his balance. He thought he knew where he was and told himself he was getting close to the cabin. The mountains made him feel small and cold, and his body shook worse than before. Think of something different, he thought. He remembered the countless times he floated the Clark Fork with Kate. They would go in the late summer. The sun would bounce off the water. The water still had a chill to it.

Don't think of the cold water, he thought. Think of anything but the cold.

He thought of the last time they had gone before Kate was pregnant with their son. It was a typical, hot afternoon in August. They left her car in Missoula and drove his pickup along the river east of the city. Then they parked and walked over the rocky bank and put their tubes and floating cooler in the water. The river was wide, and there were small trees and shrubs on one side at the foot of the mountains. They floated down the calm water and drank. Something people will do forever, he thought. No matter how far time goes, some things do not change. Like floating a river in the summer or sledding down a hill in the winter. Or loving a woman. He thought of Kate's beautiful laugh. He could see her smile and feel the sun on his neck. Everything about her was beautiful, even her gypsy soul. And the scenery was heavenly with the mountains next to the river and more mountains further in the distance. The trip had taken most of the afternoon, and the river remained mostly calm. They only floated over one set of rapids before getting out of the river. He remembered falling in at the start of the rapids and making it through without getting hurt, which had happened before. They got out, and once they made it back to the city with both vehicles, they went to the bars. He could not remember which bar they went to first. He thought it was the Draught House. He remembered getting beer and then sitting on the patio. The sun was hot, and he and Kate had both gotten burnt on the river. The beer was cold. A good cold, though. A cold that complimented the heat of the day. What was it she said? he wondered. He could hear the other people laughing. All the hipsters and hippies that frequented Missoula. He could remember where they were sitting and the table umbrella that shaded everything but his arm that held a beer. He remembered.

"I'm already tipsy, and we just got here," Kate said.

"Are you? I got a good buzz on the river, too."

"Well babe, we're having a great time then. I love this bar and this patio. It's a comfortable place."

"I find any bar comfortable."

"That doesn't surprise me with you. If there is a stereotype that's true, it's drinking like a sailor."

"Some of them don't drink."

"You drink like a fish, and all of your friends do as well."

"We're just unique in that way."

"That's a good word for you, alright. Let's walk to Main Street and find another bar."

"I thought you were happy with this bar."

"Yes, but I've seen it now and would like to see another."

"Finish your beer then, and I'll pay the check."

She was always in a hurry to go somewhere else, he remembered. She had never really changed, and neither had he. That was the funny thing about life. People can think they have changed or are going to, but they don't. In small ways, yes. But unless tried with vigor, never in ways of character.

A rabbit darted out from behind a tree and ran in front of him. That startled him.

"Where the hell have you been?" he asked with a shaky voice. "You're fortunate the circumstances are what they are. I couldn't even grip my pistol."

The rabbit would run up ahead of him and stop. Then wait for him to get closer and take off again. He was never out of sight. Ray kept on. He did not recognize anything he went passed but followed his path, so he had to have been there before. He was still cold, but the blanket had lessened his shivering, and he could feel his body heat being trapped within. His feet were the worst, and he wondered if they would come off with his boots. He made it to a hillside and saw the cabin and the smoke. It was just down the hill through the trees.

The rabbit stopped and watched Ray run by. He did not look at the rabbit. Halfway down the hill, he tripped over a dead tree branch and tumbled into the snow. When he came to a stop, he grabbed his gear and stood back up. The blanket had slipped off partly, and his body had snow stuck to it.

It's hell to get old and fall down all the time, he thought.

He continued and neared the cabin. It seemed so far away. He looked ahead as he proceeded to climb downhill. You've made it this far, he thought. He reached the cabin, and the door was ice cold on his hand as he shoved it open. The heat enveloped his body. He dropped his gear and ran straight to the stove. He opened the stove door and began to rub his hands over the fire. The heat stung his hands, but he did not care. He rubbed his whole body to warm it up. He opened the blanket around him to catch the heat. The snow on the blanket and his body melted away. He took his boots off slowly, and his feet stung as he did so. They did not come off with the boots, and he smiled at that. He placed his feet closer to the stove. As soon as he had feeling back in his hands, he started the chimney fire. The floor felt cold on his feet, and he walked like he was crossing gravel. He grabbed a towel and dried himself off. He still shivered. He sat by the fire and warmed up.

The cabin was warm. He touched his forehead and remembered his wound. There was not much he could stitch so he cleaned it and bandaged it with material in his first aid kit. He no longer shivered but his body was still chilled. The hunger in his belly had returned, and he cursed the rabbit. Foolish, he thought. I should have just fixed some more deer and been done with it. The damned ideas I get. He found the warmest blanket he had and wrapped himself in it and sat back down for a time.

He did not think of much or move at all. He was just pleased to be inside the cabin now and dry. After the partial shock had gone away, he cooked some venison and green beans. I should have made this in the first place, he thought. The food warmed his stomach and made him happier. He drank a lot of water and stayed by the fire for the remainder of the day. He reminded himself to stay awake because of his head injury. The crackle of the fire was soothing, and the flames bounced around the logs.

It reminded him of island girls that danced on the beaches in Guam. Their hips moved as the flames did. You could see what they were capable of, but you didn't know where they'd move next, he thought.

I could go for a beach now, he thought. And some island gals. Well, only if they aren't crazy. Just sit around in the sand with some rum, and the ocean water would be eighty degrees and would feel like a bath.

The thought of rum made him thirsty, so he got some whiskey. It ran down his throat and warmed everything on the way down. He took a few more pulls and set the bottle down. That stopped the chills he had, and he finally felt normal again. Besides the pain from his head wound.

The rest of the afternoon went by fast, and so did the evening. He stayed by the fire and did not go hunting again as he had planned. The wind had picked up outside and sounded like it would carry the cabin away. The snow swirled around, the wind howled, and the trees were hard to see through the white haze.

The weather had remained wild into the night, but by morning the wind had calmed, and the snow had settled. In some areas, the snow had been blown away, and not much was left. In others, it was piled higher than the day before. The sun shined, the uneasiness had gone away, and the mountain was calm and quiet. The snow had piled up against one side of the cabin and had been blown into the creases where the logs came together.

Ray laid by the fire that still burned. His neck and shoulders hurt some from carrying his pack the day before. I must be out of shape, he thought. His head was sore, but his body was warm. He was thankful for that. The first thing he thought of was breakfast and then of his Winchester. He had bought the model 70 Alaskan some years before, but he could not remember exactly when. He had left the gun at home, and for some reason was thinking about it. It had been reliable, and that was a quality he loved. He wished that he could hunt with it this trip, but it was muzzleloader season.

Then he remembered what he saw by the river. He could not figure out what it was. He knew it was not Jim, but that was the first thing he'd thought of. If I had really seen something, then what was it? he wondered.

I must have been thinking about him before, he thought. I know it wasn't Jim. He would have hollered over at me, dead or not. He must have gotten a pretty good laugh when I fell in. It is kind of funny now that I'm inside and cozy, he thought.

He had body chills and wanted food. First, he looked at his head wound. He removed the bandage and it looked like a day-old wound looks and was bruised all the way around it and down near his eye. He scrunched his eye as he cleaned it and bloody water ran down the rag. Once he was finished, he let the wound air out.

Then he got naked and used alcohol wipes to clean his body because there was no running water. He did this once a day every hunting trip and would shower when he returned home. Then he put clean clothes on and had oatmeal and toast for breakfast and coffee like he always had. The hot oatmeal felt good to him and warmed his whole body. The day was perfect for bears to be foraging but he did not think he would hunt. He thought that it would be best if he stayed in the cabin for the day so he could just keep himself warm. The day was quiet, and the cabin smelled of firewood. For having fallen in a river he was in a good mood and even more excited to find a bear than he had been before. He pictured a scene where he would kill a bear and how big the bear would be. That's all I want, he thought.

He spent the day kindling the fire and staying wrapped in a blanket next to it. The temperature had risen into the high thirties and that helped keep the cabin warm too. When he got too bored, he got out a deck of cards and played solitaire. That made the time go by, and he would curse himself every time he lost. Then he looked at a few books that had been left in the cabin over the years and decided to read some of one. He enjoyed reading when the book was a good fiction or a historical non-fiction. There was a picture in the book that had been used as a bookmark. It was Ray and some of his friends on the deck of their ship with a port city in the background. It was Pattaya, he thought. He remembered posing for that picture. He remembered the whole first day in port.

The ship was going at a slow speed, and land was less than a mile away, and the ocean still rocked the ship but not as much as the open sea. After taking the picture, Ray, Jim, and some others were down in their shop on the third deck of the ship. It was early morning, but the hot, humid air blew through the midship and down the ladder-well, into the shop. The shop was full of machines that bent, rolled, or cut metal. They stood around a weld table as they worked and talked.

"I'm glad I don't have duty on the first day in port," Ray said.

"Same here," Jim said. "And it'll be early afternoon when we get out of here. Nothing better than dropping anchor early in the morning."

"Just rub it in," Ed said. "What are you guys going to do? Go check out some temples or the Buddha or ride some elephants?"

"Hell no!" Jim said. "I can see that on a postcard or at the zoo. You can't be with any whores at the zoo."

"Well, you could take a whore to the zoo if you were a kind gentleman," Ray said.

"I'm a kind gentleman. Maybe I'll do just that."

"It's probably best to be on the ship with you two on the loose," Ed said. "I'll just hold the fort down."

"Have you guys been on Walking Street?" Tommy asked.

"No. This is our first time here," Ray said.

"It's a blast."

"That's what I've been told," Jim said.

They sat around and talked until they had to muster, which they had to do before they got their liberty to leave the ship. Their chief addressed them and then dismissed them. They left the shop and walked up a ladder-well, and then forward through two hatches and passed the post office and passed the barbershop, and then down two decks to their berthing. Everyone else in their division was showering and changing, getting ready to get off the ship. The ship set anchor in the harbor, and a floating platform was tied against it so a picket boat could ferry sailors to and from land. The ship was a gray colossal in the harbor as tiny fishing boats passed by like fish fleeing from a hungry whale. The pier was covered with cargo containers, cranes and drydocked ships. Ray, Jim and a small group headed for land. The picket boat ride took a half hour. Once on shore, they still walked with a sway. They were used to the ocean and still had their 'sea legs'.

"Always takes a bit to walk normal again," Ray said.

"Don't say that too loud," Jim said. "Someone will think the Navy jokes are true."

"It does get awful lonely out there," Rodriguez said.

"Rod, you get lonely the minute you tell a woman bye," Ray said.

"That's why I have so many."

The group of them left the pier and went down the sidewalk of the busy street. The traffic was bumper to bumper, and men on bicycles rode passed, and young kids ran between the crowd. The streets were lined with vendors and markets, and there was a jumble of noise that carried through the crowd like the wind. They walked along until they were tired of walking and looked for a cab. They could not find any, but they found a man holding a sign that said Walking Street. Ray asked him where that was and how they could get there. The man spoke Thai, but he understood what they wanted. He said some things that none of the group understood and walked between them and waved one hand in the air. Then an old pickup pulled up next to them and stopped. It was their ride. Ray told the man thanks, and they hopped aboard. The driver sped off just as everyone sat down. It was the fastest driving any of them had ever seen through city traffic. The driver weaved between honking cars and slow bicyclists, and the sailors sat in the back and watched the ship disappear. They got to the street and paid the driver. The street was lined with bars and women that worked the bars. They hollered at the passing sailors and told them to come get drinks in the best English they could. That is what they did. They walked in the first bar that caught their eye and sat down for a drink. They stayed at that one bar for the rest of the afternoon. Later, they ate some food and continued to watch the ladies walk by them with smiles. They talked about anything and everything that young men talk about. The evening approached and they were all buzzed.

"I think Rod and I are going to go look for some women somewhere else," Jim said.

"What's wrong with here?" Ray asked.

"I know of a better place," Rodriguez said.

"We'll wait here. Don't be long. If you are, we'll

head back to the pier without you. We've got to be back by midnight you know."

"Yeah, we'll be back," Jim said.

The two of them left, and Ray stayed with the group. They had a swell time and drank and laughed the day away. Each one of them, including Ray, took a lady to one of the back rooms at some point in the evening. The sun went down, but the open bar was still warm, and the cold beer was cheap. They drank shots of whiskey and played darts and cursed one another. The ladies laughed at them because they treated them well and paid them well. The night came, and they got drunk and kept drinking. Five older British men walked in and looked at them and sat down. They had most likely been in the Royal Navy and grown fond of the place, so they moved to Thailand after their service. The American sailors paid them no mind but were loud, drunk, and young. Ray walked to the head, and one of the older men bumped into him with his shoulder.

"What the hell?" Ray said.

"Piss off."

Ray was never one to fight sober, but when he got to drinking too much, he was known to have a temper and a short one at that. He stepped back towards the man, and one of the others pushed him. Ray shoved the man's hand away and swung a quick right hook into his left cheek and then a quick left into the other man's nose. By then, Ray's four friends had stopped what they were doing and were running toward the fight like bulls down a street full of people. Ray took a jab to his nose and gave one back and then tangled with the man over a table and onto the floor. By then, the others had collided with the other four, and tables and chairs were sliding, and beer was spilled over the bar. The ladies in the bar had seen fights before and were watching the whole thing. The men scuffled for a while longer and then slowly broke the fight up themselves. The way a fist-fight should end. None of them were kicked while they were down, and no weapons were used. There were bloody noses and lips and bruised knuckles, and one chair had been broken. The fight did not last very long though, and no one had called the authorities. Ray picked one of the British men up off the floor and shook his hand.

"You hit pretty good for an old man," Ray said.

"And you've got quite the right hook for a yank."

"You chipped one of my back teeth. I hate the damned dentist."

"Sorry, lad. You got me well enough, too."

"Let us buy you fellas a round."

"Perhaps we should have done that in the first place."

"Na, we needed a good fight."

The ladies still looked concerned but got them more drinks anyhow. The sailors picked up the chairs and tables and put them where they belonged. Ray gave the broken pieces of a chair to the bartender and gave her money for the damages. His nose was bloody, but he did not mind. They stayed for a few more rounds and talked with their new friends. They compared sea stories and showed each other tattoos. The night was getting late, and they had waited for Jim and Rod long enough. They paid their tabs and stumbled their way back out onto the street. They found five bicyclists with carriages and paid the men who rode them to race one another back to the pier. The bicyclists took off, and the drunk sailors laughed as they sped down passed the streetlights and bars. They raced the whole way back to the pier without any accidents, and the sailors cheered and tipped them for their efforts. It was nearly midnight, and there was no sign of the other two. The last picket boat was on its way to the pier and would be headed back to the ship within the hour. Ray told the others to get on the boat, but they all stayed and waited. Finally, just before the boat was due to leave, Jim and Rod showed up in the same pickup they'd all ridden in earlier. They were both as drunk as the rest of them. The group stood there and looked as though they had been awake for days. They had some bloody lips, and their hair was messy. Ray's shirt had some of his blood on it.

"What the hell happened to you?" Jim asked.

"We were defending your honor," Ray said. "Where the hell have you been?"

"We were running the town. You know that I think fighting is barbaric anyways. We went back to the bar, but you guys were already gone."

"It was getting late, and we needed to get back. We didn't want to talk to the captain in the morning."

"Well, let's go back to the ship then," Jim said. "This rocky boat ride ought to be good for the way I feel."

"Yeah, I'll probably be leaned over the side for most of it."

The night sky was dark and empty, and the pier was lit up by pole lights. They rode the boat through the choppy harbor back to the ship. The quarter-deck was quiet besides the noise of the sailors returning from shore. They made their way down to their berthing and into their racks for the night. Ray remembered hearing someone fall out of their rack shortly after going to bed. He laughed at that and at his memory of the entire day they had.

What a memory, he thought.

He looked at the picture again and then laid it down. Pictures really are worth a thousand words, he thought. He opened the book to the beginning and started to read. The morning had passed by, and he read into the early afternoon before wanting some food. He was warm and happy being wrapped in a blanket by the fire reading, but he was hungry. He had lunch and then read more, all the while staying warm. Sometimes he thought of falling in the river, and he would shake his head and be embarrassed for himself.

How did I do that? he wondered. The curiosity still had not left his mind. There wasn't anyone over the river, he thought. My mind, if anything at all. Getting so old I am seeing and imagining things.

The afternoon went on, and so did his thoughts.

The cabin was quiet, and the sun shined outside. He took the rounds that had gotten wet out of his pistol and threw them away. He cleaned the gun and put it back in his holster. Then he removed his knife from the sheath and spent a long time sharpening the blade. His hands glided the knife's edge over the damp stone, over and over. The sharpening made the only sound in the cabin. The night came, and he thought of nothing but black bear.

The night passed by, and the coals of the morning fire glowed, and he went outside to get some more wood. The day was warming and serene. The stubborn snow that had not melted clung to his boots. It's a good day for the hunt, he thought. He gathered some wood and went back inside to kindle the fire.

He had his breakfast and coffee while he read a sports article from a magazine he had brought. He did not normally read anything about sports or watch them much. Not as much as he once did. They had lost his interest over the years. He was a strong football player in his youth but never cared about it after. He thought that football had gotten ridiculous with the rules and politics. Hockey needed fights to keep the scorers healthy. He hated all the politics and rule changes. Baseball was fun in the playoffs. Basketball had turned into a scoring game with no defense and the fundamental rules had gone out the window. He had never watched much wrestling or mixed martial arts, but he respected both sports. Maybe I'll get into watching racing, he thought. It had always seemed boring to him, but he had not really tried to watch it. Or golf, he thought. It's not too fun to watch but it's fun to play. It would be a nice sport to make a fortune playing.

"I should have been a professional hunter," he said. They could have listened to me whisper for a bit and then fall in the damned river, he thought. That would attract fans.

After breakfast, he cleaned and bandaged his wound again. It had started to heal but the bruise was still evident. He checked his supplies and re-packed everything in his pack. The sun continued to shine through the window and made him positive about the day. He would wait until late afternoon to go hunt. That is when he had wanted to go two days prior, so he stuck to that plan. The cabin was lonely and quiet. Ray was used to being alone but not on trips. It was quieter than he liked it to be. He wished that Jim were there. Jim would start talking about anything and pass the time away.

The day went on, and he cleaned the cabin and moved around more than he had the previous day. He felt good and healthy and had not had any chills this day. He was thankful for that and was glad he had not gotten worse from the incident. Maybe I'll get sick in a few days, he thought. I won't even mind getting sick if I've killed a bear by then. He ate lunch and watched out the window for any activity. He saw birds and that was it. His hands were sore and stiff, so he moved his fingers in and out until the pain subsided. Damned arthritis, he thought.

The time had come, and he could not wait any

longer, he wanted a bear. The afternoon was the same as the day before, much warmer than the first day. He stepped outside with a full pack and his muzzleloader slung over his left shoulder. His face looked rough and beaten up, but he was eager. He walked the opposite way from where he had fallen into the river. He thought maybe that would change his luck. He thought about driving the four-wheeler that sat in the utility shed, but he decided against the idea.

The sound of the four-wheeler would be too loud the way I'm going, he thought. My walking will be loud enough. If I don't find one today, I'll take the four-wheeler up the road tomorrow. Be positive about today, he thought. And you won't need tomorrow.

The snow made its own white hills around the trees. It reminded him of the rolling plains in southern Iowa. Jim called them hills, but they were much smaller than the hills in Nevada and in the mountains. Ray had gone there a few different times to visit Jim and to hunt. He always went in the fall, when the trees had shed their leaves and nature was preparing itself for winter. The pastures bordered the corn and bean fields in uniformed squares. The golden-brown stalks of corn would wave in the wind, and the deer would run. He loved to watch the deer run. He thought of one time. It was his favorite time.

They were bow hunting whitetail deer. He and Jim sat in a tree stand on Jim's family land. They had gotten to the stand before the sun rose. The weather was dry and calm, and the air was crisp. The stand was elevated at the edge of the timber, and they looked out through a cornfield that had already been harvested. Leaves littered the timber floor and drifted out into the field. The cornfield sloped some, and patches of trees grew in the grassy waterways. A creek ran along the edge of the field, and a ridgeline overlooked the timber. The two of them talked quietly.

"It's actually kind of warm sitting here," Jim said.

"Yeah, I'm just about perfect."

"I don't know how you ever talked me into being a hunter, but you did. I rather enjoy it now."

"I told you that you would. Hunting is a pure distraction. Whenever I am separated from it for too long, I yearn for it."

"You sound like a poet."

"It's from waking up early. I always talk weird when I'm tired."

"Well, the sun's coming up now. Hopefully, the deer are hungry."

The sun was not visible behind them through the mess of trees, but its light passed through the timber and could be seen up on the ridgeline.

"Legend has it that Jesse James camped on that ridge after he robbed a bank north of here," Jim said.

"No shit?"

"That's the legend anyway. Or the story. Whatever you want to call it. This would have been on the way to Missouri, which is where he was headed."

"Makes sense then. Maybe someday they'll talk about how you and I hunted down in this bottom ground."

"We'd better do something productive soon then or become outlaws."

"Nowadays you don't have to do either. So, we may have a chance at fame."

"We're just about getting too old. I don't have the hair for it."

"We'd blow the money on booze."

"That we would."

The sunshine touched the entire field now, and the frost disappeared from the ground. The morning went along fast, and the two of them talked. Ray missed the conversations they had. They sat in the stand and ate snacks that they considered their breakfast. Mid-morning came, and they had not seen a doe or a buck.

"They must smell you and won't come anywhere near us," Jim said.

"Oh yeah, what's that?"

Jim turned around and saw what Ray had already seen. A lone buck walked through the trees behind them. It was still too far away and behind too many trees, but the two of them got turned and ready. They stayed quiet and did not move much. The buck walked slowly and would stop and sift through grass. It walked towards the open field and approached the stand. Jim motioned to Ray, telling him to take the shot. He got his bow ready, and they remained quiet. The buck moved through the trees at an inconsistent pace. It walked into an opening and stood broadside of them. Ray took a moment and moved only his finger and released the arrow. It stuck into the buck directly behind its shoulder, and the buck jerked and ran off for a short distance until it collapsed onto the leaf-riddled ground.

"Nice work!" Jim said.

"That was the best I've ever shot with a bow."

"I'll say. You hit him perfect. Let's go get him."

They climbed down out of the stand and onto the crunching leaves. Ray remembered seeing the buck laying there and how excited he was to have killed it.

I would love to kill a bear today, he thought. Today is the day. I can feel it.

He walked the path of least resistance through the snow. There were more trees in the direction he took this time. He walked along on a slant and was headed downhill. The sun was behind him, and his shadow walked out in front of him. Birds made more noise than the days before, and he noticed some rabbit tracks and cursed his troubles under his breath. A valley was in front of him, and mountains were to his left. He could see out through the trees and down onto the valley. The valley had far less brush, and a river ran through it. He knew that the river ran into Dove Lake, which sat just over a small set of hilltops. He changed direction and walked towards the lake.

I kind of want to see the lake up close, he thought. It was always pretty with some snow around it.

He came to the small set of hilltops. They were treeless and peppered with rocks. Snow covered most of them, but there were tiny patches of grass here and there. The hills were small compared to the mountains but still winded him. He made it to the top with heavy breaths, and his legs burned a little. The sun hung over the trees on the horizon and bounced off the snow. That made him squint. He looked out over the hills at the lake.

"She's beautiful," he said. It gets better the closer I get, and it's better from this angle, he thought.

The lake sat a mile below in the middle of what looked like a million trees. The foliage still had color to it. Mostly green with some oranges and yellows. The lake looked like a mirror, and on the backside of it was more foothills and mountains. The mountains were all covered in snow. It would make the perfect painting, he thought. There were homes on one side of the lake that Ray could not see from higher up the mountain. There were more of them now than there had been the year before and the year before that.

I'd leave the houses out of the painting, he thought. I would have liked to have seen this place when the natives still roamed it. That would be something, he thought.

He sat on a rock and got some jerky from his pack.

It's good to rest and think about what to do next, he thought. I'll probably turn and head east again. I don't want to get any closer to the lake. Hopefully, a bear is out there somewhere resting and deciding to walk to the same place I am. It would probably look like me. Old and tired. I don't even know if I'd shoot it if it looked like me. It would be more fitting to square off with it. There's an idea, he thought. I'll find one and we'll do some hand-to-hand fighting. I'll get my knife and the bear will get what it's got. That's fair.

He laughed aloud at his idea.

"I must be concussed," he said.

He laughed more and drank some water. He put his pack back on and headed east. He followed the sloping hills over and through some passes. Then he was back in the trees again. He happened to look over and see some wolf prints in the snow. He had not seen any of those yet. He thought the tracks appeared to be from just one wolf, and he was confident in his opinion. There shouldn't be a wolf roaming this time of day, he thought. He checked to make sure his muzzleloader was loaded with his ramrod. Then he looked at his pistol cylinder and counted six rounds. He continued. Birds still made some noise. That's a good sign, he thought. He started up a hill now, so he was headed more towards the cabin. He figured it was time to make his way back, so he would loop around and keep hunting while he did so.

It's warm, he thought. The worst part about the walking is getting warm. You either stand around and get cold or move around and get warm. Nothing's perfect.

The sun was behind the hills now, and his shadow

was gone. It would be quicker on the way back since he would not be going down to look at the lake. He was not sure if he had been as far as he was away in that direction from the cabin on foot before. He kept on and made good time until he came to a steep grade. He breathed heavier, and the pack dug into his shoulders a little more. After a good distance up the grade, he came to a short cliff face. The rocks hung out like platforms up to the top but were not very steep. Reaching the top would get him back on a straight path towards the cabin. He stood at the bottom and looked up. He could walk around, but that would take longer, and the rocks looked safe and simple to him.

It's only about fifty feet, he thought. Hell, I can climb up that. The snow might be a little tricky, though.

He rubbed his beard with his hand and then started up. The rock platforms were spread out and wide. He would clear off the snow with his gloved hand before grabbing hold. He would reach and pull himself up to the next and then stand and do it again. In a few places, he would go up and turn with the crooked rocks. He had made it halfway when he stopped for a break. The climb winded him some, but he climbed well for an older man. He looked down at where he had been and then up at what was ahead.

"It feels higher from up here," he said. I must not like the heights, he thought.

Once he felt rested, he continued. The second half

was much the same as the first. He got quicker as he went and picked up a rhythm. Near the top was a break in the platforms, and instead, there were embedded rocks just large enough to grab ahold of. He paused for a moment and looked over the situation. The gap between was too far for him to reach.

"Son of a bitch," he said.

The way back down would not be all that dangerous, but he did not want to waste the time. He reached for the closest rock to grab and got a good hold. He pulled himself up and grabbed another rock. Then his foot slipped, and he nearly fell. His hands were tired now and started to cramp.

I just about fell again, he thought. Keep going.

He got his foot ready again and reached for the next platform. He got a good grip and pulled himself up. Then the rest of the way was easy, and he made it to the top of the cliff and laid on his stomach for a moment. The sun was still out of sight, and the mountainside was shadowed. He could see down the mountains where the sun still shined. He got to his knees and caught his breath, worked the cramps out of his hands then stood up and moved on.

He could walk straight back to the cabin now. It would only take him an hour or less. He remembered the area and was certain that he had never been below that rock face before. He knew that set of mountains very well. It was all public land, but he knew it like his own. He was back in thick trees. There were dead trees that had burned many years before laying around. It looks like the past meeting the future, he thought. He felt like the old burned trees. Like everything was changing, and he was not, so the new started to grow right next to him like he was not even there.

Well, someday they'll be the burned trees and feel the same way that I do now, he thought. And if I make it to heaven, maybe God will let me watch the bastards get old and obsolete like me. He laughed out loud. I ought to write some of this down, he thought.

Then a rabbit sprinted by ten yards ahead of him. His reaction caused him to unsling his muzzleloader and raise it to the ready position. He watched the rabbit as it went. I could have had you this time, he thought. He was not going to shoot at the rabbit, raising his gun was just a reaction. I wouldn't want to waste a shot with the muzzleloader, he thought. The rabbit was moving fast like it was being chased. The air was quiet, and he felt the cold on his opened eyes.

The birds are quiet, he thought.

He lowered his weapon and looked around. The rabbit was gone, and the sun was not far behind it. He stood still and listened. Then he started to walk again. The sound of his footsteps broke the silence. He had not made it far when he saw something up in front of him. It was something big on the ground. He could not tell what it was.

It might be a rock or a log, he thought. Or a dead animal. That's big whatever it is.

He walked through the trees and got closer and realized it was a dead moose. It had not been dead for too long. Its back was facing Ray. He kept walking, and then a pair of eyes looked up over the dead moose. Ray stopped. It was a mountain lion. Its ears were short, and its eyes were fixed on Ray. It stood up, and its mouth was bloody. A piece of meat hung from its teeth. Ray aimed his muzzleloader and got ready to fire. Then the mountain lion looked to the side quickly. Ray had his finger on the trigger and was about to squeeze when it turned and ran away at a swift pace. Ray watched and was impressed at how smooth it ran.

He took a deep breath and lowered his weapon. His heart was beating rapidly. He slowly walked over to the moose. He could not see the mountain lion anywhere, but he remained cautious. The moose was bigger than Ray thought he was.

"You're the biggest moose I've ever seen," he said. Well, what's left of it, he thought.

Then he heard a noise. He turned in the same direction the mountain lion had looked. There were two gray wolves walking towards Ray and the moose. Then two more appeared not far from the other two. All these predators and not one damn bear, he thought. He stood still. He looked down at the moose and then back at the wolves. The wolves were full-grown and approached him with confidence. The gray hair on their backs stood up and made them look bigger. Their coats were mixed gray and brown with white near their neck and belly. They continued to advance. They walked like they owned the territory, and Ray was an unwanted guest. He hollered and screamed, hoping he would scare them. It did not work.

I am between them and their food, he thought.

He could kill one wolf with the muzzleloader, but he would not be able to reload the weapon fast enough. The only logical idea was to use his pistol. It would be quick, and he was experienced with it. He leaned his muzzleloader against the closest tree and drew his pistol and pulled down the hammer. Then he started to step backward. He would look behind him and then back at the wolves who were walking faster than he was. The wolves began snarling and growling. Their sharp teeth showed, and drool ran down one's mouth. The moose was in the middle of the conflict now, but the wolves passed by and stayed after Ray. He was still backing up when he stumbled. He caught his balance before he fell. The closest wolf jolted and attacked. The other three followed. Ray stood straight, aimed his pistol quick and fired. The shot was loud and echoed through the mountains. It hit the wolf square in the middle of the chest. The wolf yelped and skidded to a stop in mid-sprint. Ray cocked the pistol and aimed for the next one. They were all closing in fast, and none of them seemed to care about their fellow wolf that had been killed. The next wolf was quicker than the first and closed in on Ray's position low to the ground. Ray fired. He hit the second one in the middle of the forehead, which killed it instantly. There was not much of a wince or a wine. It was just dead. Ray reloaded again and aimed for the third wolf. The last two had closed to within several feet and were at full sprint. Ray aimed and fired as quickly as he could while still getting a good shot off. His third shot hit the nearest wolf in the shoulder. The wolf barked and went head-first into the snow, leaving a messy streak of red. It was still alive, but barely. By the time Ray reloaded, the last wolf was about to lunge forward. As the wolf lunged, Ray turned and fired his fourth shot, which grazed the wolf's side. The wolf collided with Ray, and they both went to the ground hard. Ray's leg landed on a rock, and he dropped his pistol. The wolf landed on its side and scrambled quickly to its feet. Ray looked over and saw the wolf was about to attack again. Ray reached for his knife as fast as he could and spun around on his back to defend himself. The wolf lunged again and bit down on Ray's arm that he had used to block the attack. Its teeth penetrated through his clothes and into the skin. Ray took his knife and jammed it into the wolf's neck. The wolf whimpered and released his arm. Blood trickled down the knife and onto Ray's chest. The wolf was dead. Ray rolled it off him and looked around. His arm was bleeding and leaked out through the holes in his coat.

I hope that's not my vein, he thought.

He sat up and got his coat off and pulled his shirts over, away from the wound. There were several puncture wounds where the teeth had gone in.

It did not appear to have cut any veins. He was fortunate. Blood was leaking from each of the holes. The snow was now crimson around Ray and the wolf. He stuck his arm in the snow and packed it around in the hope it would stop the bleeding.

I don't believe the trouble that I am having, he thought.

He looked around at the scene that had just played out. His heart was beating faster, and he took deep breaths to slow his breathing. The third wolf he shot was still alive, but hardly breathing. The other three lay silent and still. Ray had not wanted to kill them. But the situation was to kill or be killed. He was happy to be on the former end of the fight. He did not know why they had attacked him after he backed away from the moose. There was plenty of food there for them to eat, he thought.

"I guess I looked too tasty," he said.

He was a little shook up from what had happened and was still trying to gather himself. The night approached. The adrenaline began to wear off, and he felt the pain from his arm and leg. He would have a bruise from the rock that he landed on. His arm would hurt like hell, and he expected that. He laid back down with it in the snow. He looked up at the sky. The trees above him had lost some of the snow from their pines, and the setting sun had caused the sky to turn orange with swirls of purple through it.

There's that color again, he thought. It's odd. The countless times I've been up here, and this is the only time I've seen it like that.

He laid in the snow a bit longer and calmed down some. He pulled his arm out of the snow, and it had stopped the bleeding. He got his small kit out and cleaned and wrapped it up the best that he could. Everything he did to it caused a sharp pain shooting up his arm. He took it well, though. He grabbed his pistol off the ground and stood up. Then he walked over to the wolf that was still barely alive and shot it in the head. He cleared the five shells from his pistol and put five more new rounds in their place.

"Well friends," he said. "That was an aggressive fight we had. Maybe under different circumstances, we could have worked this out peacefully."

The day disappeared, and the mountains were silent. The moon was bright though, and the stars dotted the sky. With the moon, stars, and the snow, it was relatively light. He did not know if he should limp back to the cabin or build a fire and rest. The temperature had warmed some, and he thought it would continue to do so. He had some warm gear in his pack. He also did not like the idea of leaving the dead wolves and wasting them, but there was not much he could do with them. Especially in his condition.

How have I gotten into this condition? he wondered. I just had to go on this trip is how. Oh, what else would I be doing? This is all I would be thinking about. I would be sitting at home cleaning one of my guns or reading about bears, wondering why I hadn't gone. Jim could have been here, but he had to die. You know I don't mean it, Jim, he thought. I know I need to suck it up and figure out what I'm doing.

He decided to get away from the dead animals so he would not have to see any more live ones that might come for food. His leg hurt worse, and he limped off, making his way toward the cabin. He would stop if he had to, but he was going to try and get back. He walked half as slow as normal and made different tracks in the snow from his one leg that did not lift all the way out.

The whole landscape was visible from the bright night sky. He could see down through two of the valleys he had walked earlier in the day. The pain in his arm became worse than the pain in his leg, which made it easier for him to walk, but harder for him to continue. He wanted a fire. He thought that the night was fair enough to sleep in, so he scrounged for some wood. He found chunks of fallen trees that were dead and used them. In his pack were matches and some old newspaper shreds that he kept for that specific reason. He used the newspaper, some twigs, and pine needles he found under the snow to get the fire going. The fire did not want to catch the larger chunks of wood, so he kept relighting it and blowing on it. He figured that the wood was too wet. After he tried for a few more minutes and added more twigs and needles, he got the chunks to burn. Then he found more and added them onto the fire. Once he got it good and going, he looked for more pieces that he could add in the night. There was plenty to be found. He sat his pack down carefully with his arm and got some jerky and water out.

"I'm going to get thin if I keep having days like this," he said.

The fire warmed him up and partially took his mind off his pain. As did the food and water. He saw a bird in a tree that kept moving its head up and down over a branch and it reminded him of a prairie dog.

He remembered a time that he went prairie dog hunting. It was a Fourth of July weekend that he spent in North Dakota with John Collins. He called him Big John. John was six feet four inches and was a sturdy two hundred and forty pounds. He was a rancher southwest of Bismarck and was a good friend of Ray's. They spent an afternoon hunting the prairie dogs on his land and the night in Bismarck for the Independence celebration. Ray had never hunted prairie dogs before then. They drove out to the edge of a 'prairie dog town' and set up their rifles on bipods on the ground. The prairie around the town had been grazed some by cattle. They had gotten good rain that summer and the grass was a darker green than usual, but still had a tan color to it. The rolling round hills kept on for miles like a desert of grass. A lone barbed wire fence stretched across the crest of a hill above the town. The town was barren and covered roughly ten acres. Small mounds with holes in the middle dotted the town. A couple of prairie dogs ran across the ground and went down a hole.

"Just look through the scope and you'll see some

pop their heads up out of the holes," John said. "Let me know before you fire."

"How long will they keep their heads up?"

"It depends. Some will even come out and sit on the mound for a while."

"There's one. I'm going to fire."

"Go for it."

The rifle rang out through the prairie. Dirt and sand kicked up in the wind where the bullet hit. It hit in front of the mound and the prairie dog did not move. Its head stayed where it was.

"I missed it and it didn't move."

"Yeah, they'll sit there till you get really close or hit em. And you'll know when you hit em."

They kept shooting and waiting for more to show themselves. John talked about the ranch and Ray listened. It was interesting to him, and he learned a lot.

"These damn prairie dogs are varmints," John said. "They ruin all the ground they come across, and they keep moving and building underground. They're a pest. Had a calf break his leg this year in one of their holes."

"I'm trying my best to hit one."

John laughed. "Don't you worry. You'll get one."

They waited for a short bit for more prairie dogs to come out. The wind was steady, and the summer sun was hot. Ray looked through the scope and took deep, slow breaths. Three prairie dogs popped up in the same vicinity, and he picked the middle one, which was the closest. It stood up and got up completely out of the hole and sat on top of the mound. Ray steadied his aim.

"Got one ready to shoot."

"Go for it."

He shot and hit the prairie dog, blowing it into pieces.

"I got it!"

"Oh yeah. I saw that come apart with my naked eye. Nice shot."

"Do you go out and make sure you hit one ever?"

"You can, but you usually can't find any trace of them. The bastards eat each other."

"Do they really?"

"You bet they do. They'll drag the dead ones back down into the holes. I guess when they're tired of eating grass, a little meat sounds good."

"You learn something new every day."

They stayed on the prairie for a few hours. Then they packed up and drove back to John's house. He remembered it was a hot and dry day.

I could go for a hot and dry day after this trip, he thought.

He reached in his pack and pulled his thermal blanket out and wrapped himself up and laid down beside the fire. The blanket felt good to him, and he was relaxed. The second time this has come in handy, he thought. He kept his pistol by his head and his knife in the blanket with him. He watched as an owl swooped in and landed on a branch not too far from where he was. He thought that it was a Western screech owl, but he was not sure. He waited for it to make some noise so he would know, but it never made a sound.

The night was peaceful, and he made it through it without a problem, besides the pain in his arm. The sun rose in the morning, and not a single cloud could be seen. The light was just above the horizon, and it pierced through the trees. Two squirrels ran by, and he watched them pass. They ran across the ground and up into a tree and out of sight. It took him a moment to remember where he was. His arm was tender, and he tried his best not to put any weight on it. He did not want to sit around any longer, so he put out the remaining embers that burned in the fire, and packed his gear and grabbed his muzzleloader, and headed towards the cabin. He looked at the tree that the owl had landed in, and it was gone. He could feel the bruise on his leg, and it hurt much worse now. He limped on. The snow had started melting off the trees, and water ran down their trunks. The snow was still deep around the bottoms of the trees and on sidehills and near large rocks. He looked forward to seeing the cabin and resting inside. He came to a gap in the trees and could see a long distance down the mountain.

This is the spur that the road crosses, he thought. The road should be right up ahead, and I can just follow it to the cabin.

The road was right where he thought it was. The snow on it had not been touched by any vehicles, only animals. He got to the shoulder and then followed it as he had planned. It ran uphill for the entire way to the cabin, flattening out in a couple of areas and then climbing again. It was a winding road and never went straight for very long. He walked on and on and finally reached the cabin.

He walked in and took his pack off. It was heavy and felt good for him to get rid of the weight. He rested on the couch near the fireplace. His forehead and cheeks were dry, and his nose was red. He lay there with his hurt arm up in the air against the back of the couch. The sunshine lit up the inside of the cabin. It was warmer than he expected it to be, and he hoped it would stay warm throughout the day and the next. He would have a better chance of finding a bear if that was the case. The thought of leaving the cabin to go home had not even crossed his mind. He could use medical care for his injuries, but that could wait. The hunt was all that he thought about. Although the days had been rough on him and he had not even seen a bear. He figured that he was due a good day. Nature was unforgiving. It was not a game and he respected it for that reason. He did not feel that he was owed a good day, but it was simply going to come if he did not give up.

The morning went by, and he laid on the couch for most of it. He thought about how the day would go. He was more confident than he had been on the previous days or any hunt for that matter, and he did not know why. He believed he would get a bear, and the thoughts of killing one filled his head. He was not bloodthirsty. He was just anxious and ready for something good. It had been too long since he had had something to celebrate. He stood up and limped around inside the cabin.

He had forgotten about the wound on his head. If he had not looked in the mirror, he may not have remembered to take off the old bandage. He took a moment to look it over. It had begun to heal quite well. The skin on both sides of the cut had started to form together. The bruise had gotten worse, though. He took off his trousers and looked at his leg. The bruise covered the back of his thigh and spread down towards his calf.

"I look like Jeremiah Johnson after a rough day," he said. I won't even be able to return to civilization after this, he thought. That would be okay, though.

His arm looked worse than he hoped it would. The bite marks had turned purplish and hurt to touch. He had used alcohol to clean the wound the night before. He cleaned it again and let it air out.

At least it's my off-hand, he thought.

He ate a big lunch of steak and vegetables. The steak was usually saved until someone had tagged an animal. He even had some canned fruit with his meal. He had fought off four wolves, and he figured that was worthy enough. He still could not believe he had done that and had to remind himself it had happened. The afternoon went on. He moved around the cabin doing random things. After he had checked his pack a few times, he checked it again.

He cleaned his muzzleloader and looked through the scope. He cleaned his guns quite often when he was bored. Not just when they needed cleaning, but whenever. It was smart to keep them clean, and he enjoyed the task. It kept his mind and hands busy. The gun felt good in his hands. It was the only muzzleloader he had ever owned, and the only one he had ever used. Muzzleloaders were more of a nuisance to him, but he used it quite often because quite often, it was law. He would much rather use a conventional rifle. He did enjoy the smoke a muzzleloader blew out when fired. It made him feel like he was in the old days when they used muskets.

I'll be damned, he thought. I am Jeremiah Johnson. Out here in the mountains on my own, just trying to survive. Well, and trying to kill a bear.

He finished cleaning the muzzleloader and loaded it. Then he made sure his gear was packed again. He looked at his wounds one more time and rebandaged them. His leg would remain sore, but he would manage. The sun was still out, and the day was calm. It was the best day he had seen since he had been there.

"I'm going to get one today," he said. The conditions are perfect, and I'll make it happen no matter what I must do, he thought. Kate would think I'm a fool for not going home and to a hospital. Don't think of her, he thought. Focus on the hunt.

"I can tend to my wounds after," he said.

It was still early afternoon, and he was geared up and ready to go. Getting to where he wanted to be would take some time, so he was leaving earlier. The gear felt light to him, and he paid no attention to the pain he had felt in his leg and arm.

The air was the warmest it had been, but still cool, and the very light breeze swept through his beard as he stepped outside. He was going to take his four-wheeler up the road and start into the hunt from a different spot. He opened the shed and got on the four-wheeler. It started, and he was on his way. He smiled like a kid driving one for the first time. He sped out of the driveway and up the road. Snow and water kicked out from behind the tires as he went. The four-wheeler exhaust echoed off the passing mountain. He zipped around each corner like he always did. The road reached a peak and then went downhill and passed a driveway. He could not see the house, but he had been down the drive and met the owners once before. That was the nearest house to his cabin. He picked up speed down the hill and around a corner. The road went on and curved multiple times before he could see the break in trees where he intended to park. The wind rushed against his face, and although the air was brisk, it was fresh and felt good to him. He came to a stop and got off the four-wheeler. It was splattered in mud and rock, and he was too, on his legs and boots.

He stood where he parked and looked up ahead. The gap in the trees was a football field wide and twice that size in length. The gap was not barren though. Some trees stood alone, and some were in small patches. Rocks and boulders were scattered about and so were dead and fallen trees. There were targets set up at different intervals on standing trees. The area was flat but climbed into a steady grade that lead up into the mountain. He could see the top of the mountain clearly.

He started across the target range. He wanted to reach the shoulder up the hill ahead of him and then wrap around onto the other side. That way he could walk into the wind and downhill towards where he thought there could be bear. The sun could not be seen. It was hidden behind a taller mountain but would be visible once he got higher up and around the hill. There had been someone out in the snow before him.

They must have been shooting the targets, he thought. Hopefully, it wasn't today. They might have scared my big bear away. I'll walk far enough from here though that it won't matter. I'll try to get up there somewhere for a good vantage point, he thought.

He started up the grade and breathed heavily as it inclined. The walk up was slow and steady. His boots crunched in the snow, and there were a few birds making noise as well. The whistles were comforting to him. The soft drone of an engine hummed in the air, and he looked around for it. A plane flew overhead, and he could barely make out what it was. It was a small plane.

"Probably just a sightseeing plane," he said. Maybe they can spot a bear for me and let me know where it is, he thought. Or maybe they're trying to get a good look at me. I'm like Bigfoot around here. Old and hard to find. They could get a picture and show all their friends back home, he thought.

The plane passed over the mountain and out of sight. Ray neared the shoulder of the mountain. He was ready for a break. He was always in good walking shape, but the years had caught up to him some, and he knew that. I still get around better than most, he thought. He could manage to walk a good distance up and around any terrain. He had been doing it for so long he was used to it. The air had gotten thinner since the beginning of the walk, and he was a lot higher than the cabin now, and he took a rest on the flat ground. He could see the four-wheeler and the entire route of the way he had walked. Once he caught his breath, he began to walk around the shoulder. He walked out of the mountain shadow and into the sunlight, like the flip of a switch. There was hardly any snow as he walked around toward the northwest. He walked between short evergreens and cursed how close they were to one another. He got through the patch, and as he walked into a clearing on the crest of the hill, he could see for miles. It was like someone had just painted a new scene in front of him. Mountains towered above him to his left, and a valley filled with green trees and snow-covered ground laid before him. He could see a river that looked like two S shapes connected to one another. He did not know for sure which river it was, but he was nearly certain that it was the Bison Horn. He had fished in the Bison Horn many times in his life. He stopped and took out his binoculars.

"Let's look for a bear," he said.

If I don't see a bear with these, maybe I'll see some random ladies that are out looking for me, he thought. That'd be the day. I'd be down this mountain in a heartbeat and probably forget all about hunting.

He laughed and scanned the view slowly.

There's probably more of a chance at seeing Bigfoot than any women looking for me, he thought. I might die laughing if he went flying by on my four-wheeler.

He laughed again at himself.

"What was that?" he asked.

He moved his binoculars back where he had just looked. He had seen something move. He focused on some fir trees and saw a rock. He kept looking around in the same area.

It had better not be Jim again, he thought. Or myself for that matter.

"There it is," he said. "You beautiful bear."

He tried to be quiet with his voice. It was a boar black bear. Exactly what he had been looking for. It walked between the trees where he first saw it move.

It looks big, he thought. It looks like it could be seven hundred pounds from up here. I don't even know what the record is, but it has to be flirting with it. I'd better get closer before making assumptions, he thought. There's no way the bear is that big.

"It's probably a cub and I'm being overdramatic," he said.

The bear was downhill from Ray a good distance. It would take him some time to get within range. Ray looked back at it through the binoculars. It was standing still and looking around. It walked up to a tree and stood up on its back paws with its front paws against the tree and looked up. It was massive on all fours and looked like a giant when it stood like that. Ray looked for the best possible route that lead down to the bear. He found a favorable path and kept his eye on the bear. He put his binoculars away and started down the slope.

He walked quickly, but quietly. He tried his best not to lose the bear, but in certain spots, a tree would block his view, or the bear would blend into its surroundings. He kept walking and looking. The way down flattened out, and he knew that he would lose sight of the bear for a moment, so he jogged down and over the crest. He could not see it anymore.

Where had it gone? he wondered. It couldn't have gone far, he thought.

Ray hurried around a group of boulders and stopped at the edge of a cliff. He got out his binoculars and looked for the bear. The area was covered in rocks and snow. There were no trees. The cliff hung out over the rocks below. He could see a rocky path that lead up to a stream that ran slowly down the mountain. Across the stream was a meadow. The grass was visible through the snow, and trees sprung up here and there. Then the forest started and covered the land down into the valley.

Ray could not find the bear anywhere he looked. It was around some trees when he first saw it and then moved closer to the forest by the stream. He figured that it had gone into the forest. He hoped it was just moving around and had not gotten spooked. He looked for a while longer and then stopped. Seeing the stream made him thirsty, so he got a drink of water from his pack. It was not far around the cliff and down to the stream.

The rocks would be hard to navigate, but I could be to the forest's edge in fifteen minutes, he thought. I should be able to find it once I get down there.

The rocks were sharp and jagged-like he was walking over small mountains. The snow made them slick as well. His leg fell between two of the rocks and skinned his shin. He cursed for a moment but continued down and over the dangerous obstacles. He could hear the stream as he got closer. He got better at maneuvering the rocks as he went and reached the stream with no more mishaps.

The water was ice cold, and he used it to wash the blood from his shin. He had just skinned it, and it bled only a small amount and nothing serious. It's just par for another day on this hunt, he thought. He stayed along the stream as he walked through the meadow, and he slowed down for a moment to look for the bear. The stream trickled along, and that was the only sound he could hear. He got on one knee for a moment and felt the strain on his bruised leg. The muscle pulled and was tight. I have got to find it, he thought. I've got to be patient too.

The meadow was lightly covered with snow, and the short grass stuck up through the snow in patches. He stood up and walked into the light breeze and followed the stream.

Maybe I'll smell the bear first, he thought. That would be handy. Then I could get a good shot at it.

He reached the forest and looked for any sign of the bear. He kept his gun ready and paid close attention. The walk had been long, and he felt the strain on his body. The trees were quiet. He saw some fresh bear droppings and then some tracks in the partially melted snow. He knew he was going the right way. He picked up his pace while still being as quiet as he could be. The trees were close together, but he could still see through them well enough. The bear tracks would disappear in the grassy spots for several feet, and then he would find them again.

I've got to be gaining on it, he thought. I've got the jump on it, and maybe it's as old as me and can't move very fast. Though I'm moving quite fast for an old man.

The bear's trail wandered around aimlessly and then turned and made a straight path. Ray could tell that the bear had begun to jog by looking at the tracks. He followed and tried to stay downwind. He could hear something ahead. The noise got closer as he walked.

Sounds like a waterfall, he thought. I don't remember the river being this close, or any falls being around either.

His hearing did not deceive him, and he could see

the flowing water of the Bison Horn River. The falls were downstream, and he could hear their constant rumble. The bear tracks disappeared but were last headed towards the river. I hope it didn't smell me, he thought. He walked up near the edge and looked around. There was no bank to the river. The snowy grass led up to the rocky edge, and the edge was flat with the river. The current was strong, but the water was calm. It looked like a mirror on a conveyor belt. The falls were in sight now. The edge of the falls was decorated with scattered rocks, and they broke up the water's mirror-like stillness as it crashed against them and spilled over the falls. He searched the shoreline for any signs of the bear. There was a broken branch on a tree near the water.

That could be its doing, he thought.

Ray walked along the river towards the falls. He could not see the bear anywhere. The noise of the falls picked up. He could barely hear himself think. His feet started to hurt some and so did his back. That happened to him whenever he spent the day walking anymore. He did not mind.

"I've got this bite wound and head wound, he thought. It wouldn't be fair if everything else didn't hurt. It's not bad anyways. Don't be a pussy.

He neared the falls and then he saw the bear. It was directly across the river, and it had walked back out of the forest and towards the river. Ray stopped and so did the bear. They looked at each other. The bear had a shiny black coat and claws to match. Its eyes were still and somber and were fixed on Ray. Its cheeks sunk around its brown nose, and it stood on all four legs like a sculpture.

You are a giant, he thought. You don't even look real.

The bear was within range, and Ray unslung his muzzleloader. His shoulders were sore, and his legs felt shaky. The gun felt like a part of him as he put it to his shoulder. His heart was pounding. The bear watched Ray's movements but did not move itself. Ray looked through the crosshairs at the bear. He noticed some gray in its fur and that a chunk of its ear was missing. Then the bear turned and showed Ray the whole side of its body. Ray paused for a moment, and the bear turned and looked at him again.

Why haven't I shot yet? he wondered. Now's my chance. That is the biggest black bear I've ever seen.

He remained fixed on the bear, and the bear on him.

Why hasn't it run off yet? he wondered. Perhaps it wants to be killed. It does look old and beat up. Kind of like me. Maybe it's alone like me. I did say I would fight it with just my knife. To hell with that, he thought.

The bear turned its head back towards the forest and looked as though it was about to walk away.

"No hard feelings," he said.

He relaxed and squeezed the trigger. Smoke rose from the gun, and the shot rang out. The bear jumped back and let out a grunt. It stumbled but stayed on its feet and then ran up into the trees and out of sight.

"I got him!" Ray said.

He reloaded his muzzleloader and let his heartbeat slow down.

I don't even know where I hit it at, he thought. I wish it would have fallen where it stood. There is still some light left in the day. If I can get across the river, I can get to the bear shortly. Hopefully, it didn't make it too far, he thought.

He looked up and down the river. He did not know where the bear crossed or he swam.

"I'm sure not going to be swimming again," he said.

He looked at the rocks that lay across the river near the edge of the falls. The water was not very deep. It was clear, and the bottom was visible. Most of the rocks were relatively flat and showed enough of themselves for him to step on while staying dry. He walked over by them and looked over the falls. It was more of a drop than he had imagined.

That's at least forty feet, he thought. I really don't want to take another bath, but I want that bear.

At the bottom of the falls, the water panned out and then slowly bottlenecked back onto its path. The trees were further from the water than they were above the falls, and the grass had shed most of the snow. Some clouds had gathered above the mountains, and the sun peeked over the trees at Ray like it was curious at what he would do next.

If I don't go across now, I'll never find the bear, he thought. Find some courage, old man. He stood at the water's edge and listened to it for a moment.

He looked across at his possible path and picked his first rock. He began. His foot found solid rock and he stepped forward with his other, going from one rock to the next. The water would touch the top of the sole of his boots but would not go any higher. He moved along well. He reached a point where less of the rocks showed. He was worried about slipping or losing his balance. The water bounced into the rocks and poured across them like the deck of an old wooden ship. He stepped cautiously to the next one and stood on it with both feet. He could see over the falls and down at the water crashing below. He was well over halfway across the river. He concentrated and kept on going over the wet rocks. The edge of the river was only ten feet away, and he sped up some. He bounded across the last three rocks and jumped onto the dry land.

"Wooooo!" he said while holding his arm up in the air like a boxer who had just won a fight.

He looked up into the forest and then back at the river he had just crossed.

One step closer, he thought. I'll have to cross back with the bear, though.

Then he walked over to where the bear had been standing when it was shot. There was some blood splatter on the rocks and in the snow.

I for sure hit it, he thought. Now I've just got to follow the blood.

First, he stopped and took a rest. He took a long drink of water and then stepped over to the river and dipped his bottle in to fill it back up. The ice-cold water ran over the bottle and down his hand. He ate some dried fruit and jerky while he sat next to the river. He looked at the trees.

Somewhere in there that bear's dying, he thought.

He stood up and followed the bear's path. There was not a constant trail of blood on the ground, but enough to follow. The river was behind him, and he was surrounded by trees. He walked downhill towards the evening sun. The downhill was easy on his legs, and he realized how tired of walking he was.

The blood trail went on for a while, and then he could not find where it went. He looked all around and did not see the bear anywhere. He looked among the sticks and snowy grass on the ground for any blood or tracks. He listened, but nothing was heard. Then he saw smeared blood on a tree. It appeared the bear had brushed against it while on his way up and over the hill ahead.

I can't believe the bear made it this far, he thought. I've come quite a long distance from that river. That old bastard has got some will.

He walked up the hill and made it to the top. There was deeper snow on the brow, and another hill started. He saw the bear's tracks in the deep snow, and they lead up the next hill. There were only drops of blood now, and they were off to the side of the tracks. He slung his muzzleloader and undid the strap on his pistol holster, then walked up the hill. The ground flattened out at the top but was still at a slight grade. He could see the tracks easier than he could at the river, but he still had not seen the bear since it took off. He kept climbing, and his breathing got heavier with each step. The snow would hold as his foot landed, but then collapse as he pushed off for his next step. That slowed him down and made him tired. Where the hell is that bear? he wondered. He was worn out, but he told himself that the bear was too, so he did not stop.

He made the top of the hill and saw the bear running down in front of him. The bear reached the bottom at the foot of a large peak and squeezed between two trees and went up a rocky slope. Ray took a deep breath and jogged down the hill after him. He kept his hand on his holstered pistol the whole way down and passed between the two trees that the bear did. He looked up ahead and saw the bear before it went out of sight around a bend on the path. Ray started up what he thought to be a goat path. The path was powdered with snow and lined with rocks of all sizes.

This is the chase of a lifetime, he thought. I'm going to get this bear.

He made it to where the bear had been last, and he jogged around the bend. If it's as clever as I am, it's setting a trap, he thought. I probably shouldn't be chasing it, but I don't want to lose it. The path went in every direction but was continuously rising. The right side opened, and he could see for miles. The sun was all but gone, and that same purple and orange tint misted over the tree-lined valley beneath, which looked like waves coming towards the shore. He smiled at the scenery, and it took his mind off the bear for but a moment. He was breathing hard, and every muscle in his body was tired. His head wound burned from the sweat that ran over it, and his arm ached. He looked at the valley once more and then at the rounded edge of the path he was on. Over the side was a steep drop covered with small gravel-like rocks, and further down were boulders accompanied with trees that had found the oddest of places to grow. All in all, that fall would hurt a little, he thought. The goat path got steeper, and he breathed heavier, and his face looked hot and exhausted. He saw blood on the path, and it reminded him of what he was doing.

It's got to be running out of the stuff, he thought.

The path widened, and trees sprung up in a patch as he got to a flat spot and stopped and listened. He could only hear his breathing. He looked for more blood but did not see any. The color no longer laid over the valley, but instead shot straight up the horizon like fireworks. He stared at it, and it made him think of a New Year's Eve night he had spent in Saipan. Those damned fireworks, he thought. He had just returned from leave and was with his friends in the tourist area of the island.

"Come out back," Pete said.

"I didn't even know there was a back door," Ray said.

"Yep, follow me."

The bar was packed with tourists, locals, and sailors, all celebrating the new year. Balloons covered the ceiling, and banners hung over the bar. The chatter of the crowd sounded like one continuous hum. The two of them pushed their way through and out the back door of the bar.

"Look at these," Pete said. He pointed at some firework tubes set up on the concrete.

"Where did you get those?"

"Bought them down the street. They were kind of expensive. Hopefully, they're worth it."

"Is it already midnight?"

"Just about. I told the other guys to go out to the front of the bar and watch."

"Let me set those two up," Ray said. "Did you get those others set up good?"

"Pretty sure. There are multiple rounds in those tubes. I was going to light them off one after the other."

"You're going to get your skinny ass shot off too."

"That's what I got you for."

"I'm no corpsman."

"I mean, to make sure I don't do anything stupid."

"I think we're passed that."

"No kidding. I'm lighting them."

"I'm standing back."

Pete started the first fuse and then went to the next one and so on. By the time he got to the fourth tube, the first one went off, sending the shot up over the buildings and into the night sky. Ray stood by the back door, and his head nodded as he watched each shot that went up. All the fuses were lit, and half of the tubes were firing when the second tube shot and tipped over. It fired its next round into the third tube, bouncing off and bursting down the alley.

"Oh boy! Not Good!" Pete shouted as he ran for cover.

Two more tubes tipped on their sides and pointed directly at Ray and the bar. He ran for the nearest cover, which was a dumpster, and dove over it as the brick wall was bursting with fireworks and echoing down the alley. He got behind the dumpster and watched as the entire area was lit up by each flash and followed by a tremendous bang. A bartender poked her head out the door and then immediately went back in and closed the door. Ray laughed at that and looked over at Pete hiding behind the corner of the neighboring building. They both smiled. The fireworks ceased and the alley was quiet.

"Damnit, Pete!"

"Hey, I've seen it do a lot worse than that before."

"I'd say about half of them went up, and the other half went towards us."

"Half going up is better than none going up."

"At least you're optimistic about it. I dove over the dumpster."

"I saw that. Quite impressive, really."

"Let's go around front before someone comes out here."

They got around the front side of the bar, and the crowd was still discussing the firework display and the noise. They passed by as if nothing happened and went in and found the rest of their friends. They were as impressed as anyone and wondered what had happened. Pete told them the story with as much added detail as he could. That lasted well into the night, and the new year had begun, and Ray went to the bar for a shot.

"Already got you one," Jim said.

"Hey bud, thanks."

"I heard Pete tried to kill you earlier."

"He came close. I think he set the fireworks up wrong just for a good story. You know how much he loves to tell stories."

"That I do. I'll have to have him tell it to me. I missed the show."

"Where were you?"

"Talking to that bartender."

"I should have known."

"There's something about these brown girls."

"Now, if we were in the Midwest somewhere right now, I'm sure you'd be feeling the same way about white women. You're a womanizer."

"I'm not quite sure the exact definition of that, so you may be right, but you may be wrong."

"I'll get you a dictionary."

"I'd appreciate that. How come you're not getting too rowdy tonight? You've seemed a little different since you got back from home. Your dog die or what?"

"I think I'm in love," Ray said.

"And I'm the womanizer."

"No, I'm serious. Met her the night before I came

back."

"What's her name?"

"Kate."

"Blonde?"

"Yeah, she is."

"I knew it. You always go for the blondes."

"I do like blondes. She's different, though. I'm hoping to keep in touch with her."

"Well, I'm happy for you pal. Let us have another shot."

They got another shot from the bartender, and Jim toasted.

"Here's to new love, found in odd places and at odd times. May you have better luck than I."

"God help me."

"I think I'm in love too."

"With whom?"

"That bartender. All this talk about love. I'm going to go see if she'll take me home. Happy new year, pal."

"Happy new year. Best of luck in your endeavors."

Ray remembered that whole night. He remembered how much he thought of Kate and how much he missed her, but hardly knew her.

That was a long time ago, he thought. Why is it always the good and young memories that I think of? he wondered. Maybe when I'm one hundred years old, I'll look back on these days with fondness. He laughed.

It's just better to think of the happier times, he thought. And the present always seems boring compared to the past, until it becomes so. It's never fun going through the bad times, so it makes sense not to think of them, he thought. Only when you don't want to repeat the mistakes is it good to think of them.

He watched as the light that streaked up the sky became a solid orange and started to retreat down toward the horizon. He looked at the path ahead, and it went up along the side of the mountain. He glanced at the pocket of trees and noticed a bear print at the foot of a tree. Then he heard a groan and then another, and the noise continued. He pulled out his pistol and cocked the hammer. It's got nowhere to go now, he thought. He assumed that beyond the trees was solid rock and a dead end. He walked slowly and quietly toward the trees and the sound of the bear. His eyes shifted between the trees and the ground in front of him and then up at the sky which grew darker by the minute. I've got to be killing it and gutting it and getting back to the four-wheeler, he thought. He knew he should not be hunting after dusk, but he had put everything else aside and all he cared about was this bear. His own health and safety had taken a back seat to the bear. He followed the bear's prints into the trees and kept his pistol ready and his eyes forward. His mouth was dry, and his lips were chapped.

I could use some water, he thought. Don't think about water. The bear doesn't have water. Get your head straight.

He leaned down and scooped some snow into his

hand and put the snow in his mouth, letting it melt before he swallowed it. Then the bear's groan fell silent. Ray stopped and peeked around the trees in front of him. He still could not see the bear, and now he could not hear it either.

Is it dead? he wondered. It put up a good escape even if it's dead now, he thought. Or did it hear me and get quiet? This bear looked too rugged to die without a fight or a last stand, he thought. Out here, nothing survives to gray hair without having that violent side.

He started to walk in further when he heard a branch break. And then another. He looked quickly ahead and around the trees. He saw black fur pass between the trees ahead and off to his right. He tried to watch where the bear went, but he could hardly keep up with it. Where is it going? he wondered. He started to back out of the trees as he watched for the bear's movement. He backed out faster now and nearly tripped on a fallen branch. Then he saw the bear's face as it changed direction in the trees only twenty yards away. He was at the tree line and aimed his pistol and fired and hit a tree. The bullet would have struck the bear in the shoulder if not for the tree.

"Son of a bitch!" he said.

He cocked the pistol and aimed again. He was standing firm and well balanced on both feet. He blinked the sweat out of his eyes and then fired. The bullet grazed off another tree, and the ricochet echoed through the mountains. The bear bellowed as it turned towards Ray and reached full speed between the trees. Ray cocked the pistol and fired his third shot into the bear's shoulder. The bear jerked its body but stayed its course. Ray tried to get out of the way as he cocked the pistol and fired for the fourth time. The bear smashed into him, and they both went to the ground. The pistol was knocked from his hands and bounced into the snow. The muzzleloader fell from his shoulder, and he landed with his pack underneath him. They both laid there for a second, and then the bear groaned as it got back up. He reached for his muzzleloader as the bear bit into his back, getting ahold of mostly the material and throwing him through the air, ripping the pack from him and tearing into it with its teeth. Ray rolled and then came to an inelegant stop. He gasped for air and then coughed and groaned.

The bear did not move as if it was waiting for Ray to get back to his feet. He slowly stood up and felt the pain in his back where the bear's teeth had cut him. The bear's shoulder was bleeding down its chest and onto its paw and the cold ground below. Ray pulled his knife from the sheath and stood ready for the bear to attack. I dropped my gun again, he thought. One of the biggest rules and I've broken it damn near every day of this trip. They both stood still.

"You sure can take some rounds," he said to the bear. "Look at us. Two old-timers fighting to the death. I knew you were tough the minute I saw you, but I'll admit you still surprised me. Well, one of us is going to die. At least it's a strong death."

The bear let out a loud growl and stood up on its back legs. Ray looked behind him at the steep edge and then back at the bear. Then he let out his own growl. It was a deep scream. He could feel his arm hairs stand up and the tingle of adrenaline run through his body. Neither one of them backed down. He did not think of running away, he thought of nothing but the fight. All else had gone from his mind. The bear stood back on all fours, and Ray looked into its eyes. He saw himself in the bear and felt empathy for it.

Just like I imagined, he thought. The two of us at the end. Let it be decided then.

He gripped his knife tightly and looked intensely at the bear. Then he ran straight for it. The bear stood back up on its two legs and roared. Ray screamed as he collided into the bear and jabbed his knife into its side. The bear's arms wrapped around him, and its claws dug into his skin. The two of them went to the ground and looked as if they had become one being. Ray pulled the knife out and jammed it back into the bear several times. Blood from the bear's wound had smeared over his face and beard. The bear's claws dug deep into his side, and he let out a screeching moan. The bear rolled over onto Ray and used its mouth and picked him up and threw him again. He skidded to a halt near the edge, and the bear immediately charged after him. He got to his knees, and the bear picked him up and threw him once more. His clothes were covered in snow and blood. Everywhere on his body had been beaten up. His body hurt some, but he was thankful for the adrenaline, which helped dull the pain. I hung on to the knife at least, he thought. He spit some blood out of his mouth and then wiped it from his dry lips. Come on, you aren't done yet, he thought. The bear looked as exhausted as he was, and it stopped by the edge of the trail. It leaned on one side more than the other, but still growled, ready to fight. Ray got to his feet, and the two of them looked at each other with the same look they did the first time they saw one another, but with more respect now.

He looked for his pistol. No, I'm not going to use it, he thought. I've already shot the big bastard twice. It wouldn't seem right at this point. I'll finish it with my knife, or he'll finish me.

He stood, and his stocky shoulders drooped, and his knees had a mild bend to them. His clothes were torn up and covered with snow and blood, some of his and some of the bear's. His pack lay torn apart near the tree line, and his two guns were several feet away from where they had fallen. His face was bruised and bloody. His wound had split open. The gray in his beard had some red mixed into it now.

Darkness had settled in, but there was still a glimmer of light through the mountainside. The bear had regained its composure and looked ready to finish the fight. Ray had forgotten about the approaching night, and he had forgotten about what day it even was. He had lost his pain as well. The bear snarled and showed its teeth and then roared. Ray charged the bear without a second thought, and it did not surprise the bear. The wounded adversaries met with wild blows. The bear caught him across the chest with its claws and then stumbled and nearly fell over the side. Ray's momentum landed him on top of the bear. It growled and dug its claw into Ray's shoulder, causing him to fall back. Then Ray jolted forward and stabbed his knife into its neck several quick times. The bear made no sound. It stared at him and looked as though it had found a peaceful moment and then blinked its eyes and then closed them. Ray's hand still held the knife and blood ran down the blade, like rivers down a mountain. I've done it, he thought. He pulled the knife from the bear's neck and sat up and leaned against the lifeless body.

"We fought a good fight," he said to the bear.

He laid the knife down and sat there for a while and caught his breath and rested. He looked out over the edge like he had done before. He could hardly make out any details in the land below. His body began to hurt everywhere the bear had cut or bit him. He had lost his hat, and his hair was as messy as his clothes, which were torn, tattered, and bloody. His body ached.

It's been quite the hunt, he thought. No one would ever believe me. Even if I had pictures. That's if I even see them again. I don't even have the energy to stand.

The night was all around him and he was content.

He laid against the bear. A soft wind blew over the two of them and swept down the trail. He had gotten the bear and that was all that mattered. Nothing else was important anymore. He thought of death and where the bear might be now. He wondered if he was to follow the bear into death. That wouldn't be right, he thought. I owe it to the bear to keep going. I've got to tend to these injuries and get up and go or stay and make camp. He stood up in a slow manner and felt every wound he had earned. If I didn't feel old before, I sure feel it now, he thought.

Then, the footing on the edge of the trail gave way. The two of them fell with the crumbling ground. Down the mountain they went at a quick pace. Ray was going head over feet and hitting the ground each time with a thud. The bear rolled with ease and Ray with difficulty. They had both climbed the trail separately and were now falling together. They rolled like boulders down the steep, rocky grade. Ray could not slow his fall or change direction. He fell helplessly. He tumbled through short pines and over rocks that poked through his already torn clothing. Then, his side landed squarely on a tree stump, and he groaned in agony. After a short distance, he smashed into a tree, and his shoulder popped and he continued to fall. Once the two of them were near the bottom, they slowed some. As he started to think it was over, they went over a short drop and a branch went through his abdomen as he hit the ground. He landed abruptly and felt the pain in his stomach and everywhere. He lay face down in the snowy ground. The bear was a short distance away. I hope I don't look as bad as that, he thought. I probably look worse. He laid there without moving and noticed how dark it was in the trees. He pictured where he was in relevance to where he had looked down the mountain before. The cold swept across the ground and into his face and down his neck.

"You're still alive," he told himself.

The night grew colder, and the trees shifted in the wind. He tried to move but could not, and he wanted to sleep. I must not sleep, he thought. I will die if I sleep. Then he felt like he was waking up from a dream, like any second this would all end.

He felt a warm liquid run over his forehead and down his nose. His body was numb, and his eyes were heavy. What's going on? he wondered. He finally opened his eyes, and it took him a moment to realize where he was. He was inside his pickup that laid on its side against a tree down the edge of the road, where he had swerved to miss the mountain goats. The engine had died, and the pickup was totaled. There was an eerie quiet. The windshield had been busted, and the glass was strewn all over the cab and on his clothes. He noticed a tree branch coming through the passenger window and up through his torso. He took a second look to be sure of what he was seeing. He still could not feel a thing. How long have I been here? he wondered. Snow had blown in and wherever there was no broken glass, there was snow. He tried to move again. His face was red and cold burned, and his beard had bits of snow and glass in it. It was daylight, but he did not know what day it could be. He looked out through the missing windshield and noticed tracks in the snow. They were bear tracks. I've been chasing death all along, he thought. He had only been dreaming and had never made it to the cabin. He did not move and nothing outside moved either.

He closed his eyes and smiled.

Not bad for my last hunt, he thought.

ABOUT THE AUTHOR

Michael James Kaufman

I was born in 1993 and grew up on a farm in rural Iowa. I served four years in the Navy and returned home. I found a passion for playing guitar and writing songs, which developed into writing fiction stories. Thanks for taking the time and reading the story. I appreciate it.

MJK

Made in the USA
Monee, IL
13 May 2020